DEFENDING MY HEART

A TEXAS TORNADO ROMANCE

LORANA HOOPES

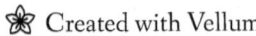

I originally wrote this book as part of a series with other authors. It was originally title Her Second Chance Forever Groom.

In March 2020, I got the rights back and had to change a few things. This new edition is dedicated to Diana who lost her battle to cancer on March 30, 2020. She was a friend, a wife, a mother, and the most amazing woman I have ever met.

Due to the quarantine of the Coronavirus, none of us even got to say goodbye. Nor will we get to attend her funeral. This dedication is just a small way to tell her how much she meant to all of us, how sad we are she's gone, and how we wished we could have been there at the end.

Life is short. Never go to bed angry and hold your loved ones close because you never know when God will call them home.

NOTE FROM THE AUTHOR

I really enjoyed getting to write a football book. I've been a football fan for years. I grew up watching the Dallas Cowboys in the 90s when they were a powerhouse team. To that end, you might notice my main character's name is Emmitt.

Emmitt Smith was always my favorite player. Not only was he an amazing running back, but he didn't rely just on his football career. He finished his college degree and that's what I found truly inspiring about him.

So, this book is dedicated to the amazing athletes who inspire us with your work ethic, with your drive, and with your never quit attitude.

CHAPTER ONE

EMMITT BROWN TOSSED in his bed, sending his sheets tangling around his feet. Figured. At least now they matched his feelings. He stared up at the white ceiling, wishing his mind could be as blank as the canvas above him. The conversation from a few hours earlier replayed in his mind like a broken record. An accusing broken record.

"You know what I've decided?" Matt Johnson, the defensive line leader asked as he lifted his glass.

Around the table, the men shook their heads. It had been a long day after attending the funeral for their owner's wife, who'd almost been like a surrogate mother to them all. She always invited new recruits over for dinner and often brought cookies to practices. She was a ray of light for the team of mostly men who often let practice and games wear them down.

Two months ago, she had been fine. Then she'd announced that she had a rare form of cancer. She'd told them all with a smile on her face and a confidence in her voice that made them believe she would beat it. But it had taken her instead.

Something in the chemo treatment had set off an infection in her body, and within hours, Leo, the owner, was taking her off life support and saying goodbye. The rest of the team didn't even get to make it to the hospital before it was all over.

"I've decided life is too short to live with regret. Diana always lived life to the fullest and though she was taken too soon, maybe we can all have the second chance she didn't get. I know I've got things in my past I wish I had handled differently, and I bet you all do too. So, I'm going to spend the time off making those things right. Who's with me?"

Emmitt glanced around at his fellow teammates. He too had things in his past that he wasn't proud of, but he wasn't sure if he was ready to face his greatest regret.

Matt held his fist over the center of the table, like he always did before they exited a huddle and ran out onto the field. "What do you guys say? How about we spend this time before Christmas making things right? Making Diana proud of us?"

Jordan White, middle linebacker, nodded and placed his hand on top of Matt's. "I'm in."

Andrew Markum, always the hesitant one, leaned back

and ran his hand across his chin. "Matt, I don't know. Sometimes it's better if stuff in the past stays in the past."

Emmitt could understand that viewpoint. The stuff in his past was more than he was sure he could face again, much less in just seven days.

Sid Lawson, strong side-back and the epitome of the strong, silent type, grunted in his usual manner but put his fist in too. "Fine."

That meant it was Emmitt's turn. He couldn't say no. It would raise too many questions, but how could he respond without having to face his shameful past? Deflection. It worked wonders on the field. Maybe it would work with the guys too. "We always have things we can ask forgiveness for."

Andrew sighed but placed his hand in as well. "You know we're always in this together." He punctuated his words with a friendly eye roll.

Matt smiled at them as he looked from one man to the other. "We make amends. For Diana."

"For Diana," the men echoed, and for a moment Emmitt was bolstered by their camaraderie. Maybe he could do this.

So, Matt had regrets, but didn't they all? Still, why did he have to recommend they go home and face them? And why had Emmitt agreed? He had spent the last few years running from his regrets, and he wasn't sure he was ready to go back yet. Had he changed enough?

He'd been working hard on becoming a better man. In fact, it was what had driven him to God, and he knew that

LORANA HOOPES

part of making that transition completely was apologizing to those he had hurt. Still, every time he thought about it, he chickened out. Mantras of *what he'd done was too awful, he hadn't changed enough,* or *apologizing wouldn't change anything* blazed in his head. Though Emmitt knew none of those were true, the words played over and over, crippling him. His kryptonite.

With a sigh, he reached for his Bible. When the demons reared up in his head like this, the only way to quiet them was to immerse himself in God's word. His fingers traced the seam around the Bible and caressed the leather. Most people at his church never brought Bibles anymore, they just whipped out their phones or tablets, but Emmitt enjoyed the feel of the physical book. The weight, the smell, and the peace it brought when he held it in his hands, when he cracked it open, and when he quieted his heart enough to let God speak to him through it. That would be hard tonight with his thoughts careening all over the place like pinballs in an arcade machine, but he would try.

Before he opened the book, he closed his eyes and took a moment to reach out to God. Emmitt wasn't even sure the prayer had words as much as a desire for God to show him what he needed. Though he didn't often, tonight he let the book fall open, and wouldn't you know it, he landed in Ephesians chapter four. He read over the words, and when he got to verse twenty-five, he knew these were the words from God.

"What this adds up to, then, is this: no more lies, no more pretense. Tell your neighbor the truth. In Christ's body, we are all connected to each other, after all. When you lie to others, you end up lying to yourself."

Oh, how fitting those words were. He was lying to himself. His teammates called him "The Reverend" or "Rev" for short because he was always praying or using scripture, but he was lying to them the same way he was lying to himself. The same way he had lied to Mia over five years ago.

Emmitt knew he had to go back. He had to make amends though he didn't even know where to begin, but that knowledge didn't tame the twisting flame in his stomach. He would just have to trust that God would open Mia's heart. At least long enough for Emmitt to apologize.

He replaced the Bible on the nightstand and turned off the light. It was going to be a long night, and an even longer tomorrow.

"CARTER, IT'S TIME FOR BED," Mia called as she turned off the sink and dried her hands. There hadn't been many dishes tonight as she tried to cook the dinner in one pot, but still she missed the dishwasher. Washing by hand every night was killing her skin, and it gave her too much quiet time to think.

"But Mom, I'm not tired." His whiny protest was punctuated perfectly with a large yawn as he looked up from his tablet. Mia was glad she and Marcus had purchased it for his Christmas gift last year. She would never have had the money to get it for him this year, and while she didn't give him much screen time, it was her saving grace when he was extremely needy. And he'd been extremely needy a lot since Marcus's death. Not that she blamed him, but she was already stressed trying to be both the mom and the dad as well as the sole breadwinner. She just had no patience left to deal with neediness.

"Uh huh, I see that, but it's still bedtime. Let's go, sport." As she ushered him down the hall of their tiny one-bedroom apartment, she wondered if life would always be like this. Five and a half years ago when she'd married Marcus, they'd had big dreams. He was going to open his own business and become a wealthy entrepreneur, but after his third business idea failed, he had given up and taken a job at the local high school. It hadn't been the fame and fortune he had hoped for, but they'd been content. At least until a drunk driver took his life.

After Marcus's death, Mia had been forced to sell their modest house and move Carter into this tiny apartment. She'd taken a job at the restaurant down the street because the tips generally paid better than a traditional minimum wage job, but she was working overtime just to keep a roof over their heads. And she missed spending time with her son. Time, she knew, was the one commodity you never got back.

She helped Carter change into his pajamas, sighing as she realized he was outgrowing these as well. He only had two pairs and both were now well above his ankles. She'd have to stop at the Goodwill soon and see if they had any a size up.

"Momma, when will Daddy be back?" he asked as he climbed into the bed and snuggled his bear. It was a question he asked at least once a week, and while Mia knew his nearly five-year old brain just wasn't capable of processing her response, she was tiring of giving it.

She brushed his hair back from his forehead and flashed a small smile. "Carter, baby, Daddy's not coming back. He had to go live with God."

"Forever?" His sad eyes pulled on her heartstrings.

"Forever, buddy, but you and me? We will be just fine." At least as long as nothing happened to her job. Or her car. Or the apartment. Or herself. That was a lot of things hinging on those last five words.

He yawned again and his eyes shut for a moment before pulling open again. "Do you think God will ever send me a new daddy?'

This was another question he asked often. "I don't know, bud. We'll have to wait and see." His eyes closed again, and she placed a soft kiss on his forehead before pulling the blanket up to his chin and tiptoeing out of the room.

Would God send another man her way? She didn't know. For the first few months after Marcus died, she couldn't imagine ever marrying again, but now, almost a year later, the thought had popped in her mind once in a while. She still wasn't sure she could marry for love, but if he was a good man, a believer, she could consider marrying to have someone by her side. A friend to share the evenings with and someone who could help her provide a better life for Carter than the one she could by herself.

She sank down on the couch, not bothering to change her own clothes, and grabbed her Bible from the nightstand. Mia knew a lot of people in her situation would have turned from God, claiming He didn't exist or didn't hear her prayers since it appeared her life wasn't improving, but He was all she had and she refused to turn her back on Him. Still, she did wish He would reveal His plan for her. She didn't think she could keep going this direction much longer.

CHAPTER TWO

EMMITT SIGHED as he passed the small sign welcoming him to Kempton, Texas. He'd thought when he left this town that he wouldn't be back. He'd even flown his parents to San Antonio the first few Christmases after he'd left to avoid returning to this dinky town. Then he had helped them move out of Kempton and retire in Florida. It wasn't the town's fault, and it hadn't been awful growing up here, but once he'd betrayed Mia, the guilt had kept him away, gnawed at his insides, and convinced him that nothing remained for him here.

In fact, he wasn't even sure Mia still lived here or that she hadn't married. Maybe she had been whisked away by some wealthy businessman or maybe she had decided to move elsewhere and was now working a dream job and making millions, but Emmitt knew that probably wasn't the case. That was a fantasy he had spun the last several years to make himself feel better about what he'd done. People rarely left Kempton. He had been the exception and not the rule.

The town had changed little, and he pulled into the one gas station to fill up and ask around about Mia. If she was still here, the attendant working inside would probably know her. Kempton was so small that everyone knew everyone else—where they lived, who their parents were, what secrets they tried to hide. Emmitt both missed and hated that part of the small-town vibe. Having people really know you wasn't something he had experienced since joining the San Antonio Saints and he missed that. But it was his own fault. He had only shared what he wanted the other men to know, keeping most of him and his shameful secret locked away. And San Antonio was a large town. He didn't even know his neighbors' names, nor did they know his. It was easier to keep his secret in a town where people passed each other without a word.

The bell above the door jingled as he pushed it open and a young clerk looked up at him. Good, this kid looked too young to remember him, but he might be too young to know Mia as well.

"You getting gas?" the kid asked.

"Yeah, forty dollars please." Emmitt pulled out his wallet and tried to sound as if he didn't need the answer when he posed the next question. "Do you know Mia Baker?"

"Mia Baker?" The kid scratched his head as his forehead wrinkled in thought. "There's a Mia who works at Manny's, but I don't know her last name. Sorry."

A waitress? Mia had always had plans of becoming an interior designer. Why would she give that up to become a waitress? "Is she about my age with strawberry blonde hair and blue eyes?"

"Uh, I think she has reddish hair. Never paid much attention to her eyes. She's too old for me, you know?" The kid shrugged as he picked up the money and placed it in the register. "Do you need a receipt?"

"No, thank you," Emmitt said and exited the gas station. If he was about to see Mia again, what he needed was a large helping of courage.

MIA GROANED as she checked her watch. She was going to be late again. Her boss was going to kill her. "Carter, let's go." She hated the angry tone in her voice, but if she lost this job, they would be kicked out of their tiny apartment and forced to move back in with her parents.

"I can't find my shoe, Mom."

Mia clenched her teeth to keep from emitting an agitated growl. This was a daily occurrence. No matter how many times she told Carter to put his shoes by the door, he never did. Instead, he kicked them off wherever he felt like it, and they were forced to go on this hunt every morning. What made it worse was that Carter was in that stage where his shoes could literally be a foot in front of him on the floor and he still wouldn't see them. And forget looking under anything. If they were under a blanket or a shirt, they might as well not exist in his world.

She began walking toward the bedroom, checking all the regular places she found his shoes as she went. Under the couch? Nope. In the hall closet? Not there either, but she struck gold in the bathroom. "I found one," she called out as she grabbed it from the floor. Why his shoe was in the bathroom was beyond her, but hopefully he had the other one.

She found him in the bedroom, sitting on the bed. Just sitting. *Don't yell. Keep your cool.* "Were you even looking?"

"Yeah, but my leg started hurting, and I needed to sit down for a minute."

This was another issue they faced nearly daily—these weird phantom pains of Carter's. She hoped they were just growing pains, but she worried they were more. Unfortunately, she didn't have the money to get them checked out, so she would just have to keep praying they were nothing.

"Okay, well, here's one shoe. Let's find the other." She handed the shoe she had found to him and then proceeded to pick up the clothes littering the floor until she found the other. After helping him get that one on as well, she grabbed his bag and ushered him to the door.

"Do I have to go to Grandma's again today?" Carter asked with a sigh as he climbed into his booster seat.

"Yes, buddy. Mommy has to go to work, and you are too young to stay at home by yourself." Mia was just thankful that her parents lived in the same town. She didn't know how they would survive if she had to pay for childcare as well. Her parents were older, but still in good enough shape to keep up with a rambunctious five-year-old most days. Still, Mia felt badly. Her parents were supposed to be enjoying their golden years and instead, they were having to help raise her son.

"All right, but tomorrow can we go see a movie?"

Mia wanted to say yes. She wished she could take him to the movies once a month as a treat, but the money just wasn't there. "How about we go to the park tomorrow morning before my shift?" At least the park was free, and on a good day, he would find a few other kids to play with and keep himself entertained for a while. Since she didn't work until the afternoon, they'd have a few hours in the morning to play.

"Okay, I guess."

She hated the resignation in his voice. This was not the childhood she had planned for him. She'd planned to stay home with him until he started school, take him to the park and on long walks. Then, once he was in kindergarten, Mia had hoped Marcus would be able to spend off time with him and that she could either return to school to finish her interior design degree or at least work a job where she could set her hours to have more time at home. Sadly, that just wasn't the hand they had been dealt.

A moment later, she pulled into the driveway of her parent's home. "Come on, buddy, let's go. I'm running late already." She chanced a glance at her watch, and her heart sank further. Fifteen minutes? She had never been this late before.

"Hey Mom," she said as her mother opened the door. "Sorry, I have to drop and run, but I'm late. Again." Mia turned to Carter and squatted down to his level. "Be good and have fun. I'll be back to get you after my shift."

He nodded, but Mia did not miss the sadness in his eyes. She sent a prayer heavenward as she climbed back into the car. "Please Lord, please help us."

CHAPTER THREE

EMMITT PULLED into the parking lot of the only family restaurant in town. There were a few other eateries in the small town, but he remembered Manny's as being the best and, according to the gas station clerk, it was possible Mia worked here. He had no idea if he would even still recognize her or if she would recognize him, but there couldn't be too many women the right age who worked here. He pulled on a ball cap and tugged it low to his eyes. It didn't always keep people from recognizing him, but it helped.

"Just one?"

Emmitt glanced up at the pretty blonde hostess decked out in white and red and nodded. Just one. He was starting to tire of hearing those words, but practice and games kept him busy. Plus, the few women he had met since joining the team were more like groupies than women he could see spending a lifetime with. The cleat chasers would appear at team parties and throw themselves at the players. A lot of the other players engaged in one or two-night stands, but that had never been appealing to Emmitt. No, he'd made the mistake of being intimate before marriage once, and he wasn't going to do it again.

"Is the counter okay?"

"Sure." Counters didn't generally have the most comfortable seats, but he could understand why they would want to sit a single customer there instead of a booth or a table that could hold more people. Plus, the place was already busy and most of the tables in the restaurant were occupied.

She led him to the chair at the end and placed a menu in front of him. A string of Christmas lights hung down from the ceiling, though they were off currently, and silver tinsel lined the back wall in a decorative pattern. "Someone should be with you shortly." Her eyes glanced around and her face took on a worried expression. "I think Mia is running late again."

Emmitt had no idea if the Mia who worked here was the Mia he had dated, but he supposed he would find out soon enough. He picked up the menu and perused the items. Though nothing sounded appealing, he decided on a burger and fries as it was typically hard to mess them up, and he was not a fan of breakfast for lunch.

"Can I get some service around here?" a man down the bar asked. Agitation covered his face and permeated the air around him.

"Yes, sorry I'm late." He recognized her voice before he even saw her enter. Her reddish hair was pulled back in a ponytail and mostly covered with a Santa hat that sat askew on her head. She was still adjusting her apron as she exited the kitchen as if she had just arrived, and she wore a harried expression on her face. Though he wasn't used to seeing her flustered, she hadn't changed a bit. Still slender and lithe, her uniform flattered her figure, and though he couldn't see her eyes at the moment, he knew they would be the deepest blue he had ever seen.

"Where's your manager?" the man growled. "I've been waiting for someone to take my order for ten minutes."

A blush bloomed across Mia's face. "I'm sorry, sir. I'll take your order right now. There's no need to contact the manager."

"Oh, I think there is," the man said snidely as he looked around the room, as if hoping to garner support from the other patrons.

"Hey, man, she said she's sorry. How about you let her take your order and I'll buy your lunch?" Emmitt spoke up. It was not the way he had wanted to tell Mia he was here, and from the angry glare she shot him, she was not pleased to see him, but he couldn't let this brute walk all over her.

The man turned fierce eyes on him, and his face

pinched together as if he wanted to start a fight, but then a greedy gleam glistened in his gaze. "You'll buy whatever I want?"

"Whatever you want," Emmitt said.

"Fine," the man returned his attention to Mia. "I'll have the chicken Alfredo bowl, a side salad, and a slice of cheesecake for dessert." He glanced back at Emmitt. "And a large coke to drink."

The man sounded pleased with himself, and Emmitt kept himself from rolling his eyes. The man's meal would probably add up to less than thirty dollars, and that was well worth the price to Emmitt to have the man quiet down.

"What are you doing here?" Mia hissed as she stopped in front of him. She kept her voice low so as not to draw attention, but he could hear the strain of emotion in it.

"I came to see you." Where were his eloquent words? Not that he'd practiced on the drive here or anything, but he usually wasn't lacking in articulation. However, with her blue eyes shooting icy daggers into him, he felt at a loss for words. What was he doing here? Did he really think she would just forgive him and want to be friends?

But that wasn't what this was about. This was about having no regrets. Whether she forgave him or not was her choice, but he would apologize and return to the team with no regrets. Well, that wasn't entirely true. If he had truly lost his chance with Mia, he would return with the regret that he

DEFENDING MY HEART

had ruined it, but he wouldn't regret trying to reconnect with her.

Her eyes flicked to the sides as if checking to see if anyone was watching them. "You saw me. Now you can leave."

"Not without eating first." Emmitt had no place to be. He'd planned to be here for a few days, apologizing and hopefully making up with Mia.

She shot him another hate-filled glare. "Fine. Let me put this man's order in and I'll be right back to take yours."

As she whirled away, the sweet scent of strawberries and vanilla wafted on the air. She was still using the same shampoo. He had always loved that scent, had loved sniffing her hair as she curled into his arms or laid her head against his chest. And he'd been haunted by that smell, which had lingered on his pillow for weeks after their one night together. Their beautiful, terrible, guilt-inducing night together.

Mia returned a moment later but though she held a notepad to take his order, her eyes did not meet his. "What can I get for you?"

"I'll take the hamburger and fries and an iced tea."

Mia issued a curt nod before turning back to the kitchen window to place his order as well. Then, without another word or glance his direction, she bustled off to take care of her other customers.

Emmitt sighed. This was going to be harder than he'd thought.

MIA TRIED to keep her composure as the lunch crowd ran her ragged, but it was so hard with him sitting there watching her. What was he doing here? Not only had she had to deal with the angry customer, but then he'd swooped in like some knight in shining armor to diffuse the situation. He probably thought the gesture alone would sweep her off her feet and she would fall head over heels for him again and forgive him. Well, he was wrong; she was not that girl anymore. She was no longer the naïve twenty-year-old who had fallen for the hometown hero and hung on his every word. No, that girl had died the day Emmitt left town for good. Without a word, without an explanation, without an apology. She'd heard nothing from him for over five years, so what was he doing back in town? And why did he want to see her?

She placed his bill down in front of him, but he made no move to pay it. He didn't seem to be in any hurry.

"How about a slice of pie?" he asked instead.

"Sorry, we're all out," she spat back at him.

"No, you're not. I can see half a pie sitting in the display case over there."

Gritting her teeth, she snatched up his bill and shoved it

in her pocket to fix. Then she grabbed a slice of apple pie from the display case and set the plate and a fork in front of him.

He picked up the fork, but made no move to eat the pie. "What time are you off today?"

She crossed her arms and leaned away from him. "For you? Never."

His lips cracked a small smile as he chuckled. "I deserve that, but I flew all the way from San Antonio to see you, and I'm not leaving until you let me talk to you."

"You said enough when you said nothing at all," she said as she moved on to another customer, but his words snagged in her mind. He'd flown all the way here to talk to her. Why? What could he possibly have to say after five and a half years? It didn't matter. She'd worked hard to build up her walls after he'd left. Even Marcus hadn't been able to completely tear them down, but he'd understood, and he'd married her anyway. And though she'd been happy, she'd never completely forgotten Emmitt. No, you never forgot your first love.

As Mia ducked into the kitchen area to adjust Emmitt's bill, Heather, her best friend and the hostess, appeared at her side. "Who is that man out there?"

"The behemoth with the wide shoulders?" Mia asked as she added the pie to the bill.

"Yes, he certainly seems to be content to stay awhile."

"Yes, he does." Mia blew out a frustrated breath.

"You know him?" Heather asked. Her eyes grew to saucers, and her hand flew to her mouth. "Is he...?"

"Yes, he is, and we're not going to discuss it." Heather was the one person who knew the truth, but Mia had sworn her to secrecy years ago.

"What does he want?"

"He wants to talk. Says he came all the way here to talk to me."

"Are you going to talk to him?"

Mia snatched the adjusted bill and whirled on her friend. "I don't know. I can't imagine it would be a good idea, but I have the feeling he won't leave town unless I say yes."

"I think you should at least hear him out," Heather said as she followed Mia back to the dining area.

"We'll see," Mia whispered before slapping the adjusted bill down on the counter in front of Emmitt again. "I can't talk tonight. I have plans when I get off." She didn't. Unless she counted picking up her son and making him dinner as plans. But Emmitt didn't need to know that.

"I only need a few minutes," he said as he picked up the bill and perused the total.

"I don't have a few minutes. Not anymore." Mia moved on to the next customer before Emmitt could say anything more. Though she was curious what he had to say, she felt it would be better if she simply sent him packing. At least then, she would not be swayed by him again.

She heard Emmitt sigh behind her, but it was not until she heard the squeaking of his barstool against the floor, signifying his departure, that she turned back his direction. Her eyes widened at the sight of Ben Franklin on the bill. "You've overpaid me," she called out to Emmitt's back.

He turned and offered a small smile. "No, I haven't." Then he walked out of the restaurant.

CHAPTER FOUR

"MOM, can we go to the park now?" Carter stood in front of her, dressed and ready. It never ceased to amaze her how he could get ready so quickly when it meant going to the park but dragged his feet when it meant going to her parents' house.

She checked her watch. It was only nine am, and she didn't have to be at work until two. If they left now, he would have plenty of time to play and wear himself out. "Okay, let's go."

As the park was just down the street, she didn't bother with driving, but she did grab her sunglasses and house keys. Though December and early in the day, the air was warm from the sun's bright rays. It had been unusually warm the last few days. Mia considered ducking back in the house for sunscreen, but Carter was already running ahead of her. With a sigh, she pushed the thought from her mind. Surely, he would be okay for a few hours, and they would leave before the worst time of day. Her mother had always told her that burning time was between eleven and two, and they would leave the park by eleven to give her time to get ready and drop him off before work.

Her feet slowed as she approached the park. A man was sitting on her favorite park bench—the one that allowed her to see all parts of the playground. Normally, she wouldn't care. She'd either join the man or sit on another bench, but a quick scan of the park showed Carter was the only kid here so far. Her protective mother instincts kicked in. He was probably just someone out for a walk who had decided to take a break, but there'd been too many stories of predators on the news lately. She wasn't about to take that chance and ignore him.

She approached the stranger, but stopped before giving him a piece of her mind. It was Emmitt, but it was too late to turn back. Carter was already on the playground. "What are you doing here?"

He looked up and smiled at her. "I was thinking about how to get you to talk to me."

"How did you know I lived around here? Did you follow me home?" Her shield was up, and even though she knew he had left the restaurant before she did the previous day, she couldn't imagine how he could have found her unless he was following her.

"No, this was one of my favorite parks growing up. I thought coming here would help me think of a way to reach you."

She sighed and plunked down next to him on the bench. She still didn't really want to hear what he had to say, but perhaps listening to him would ease his conscience and allow him to leave. "Fine, Emmitt, what did you want to say to me?"

He looked at her with those deep soulful eyes that had always sent her heart careening in her chest. Even now, she felt it start to beat faster, and as the moment drew out, she pursed her lips together to keep from urging him to get on with it.

"I wanted to say I was sorry," he finally said.

"Sorry? You're sorry? For what? For wasting three years of my life? For telling me you loved me when you obviously didn't? For leaving without a word?"

His face appeared to fold in on itself, and for just a moment, she felt badly, but it was only a moment. He'd left her, not the other way around. She'd been the one left wondering what had happened, what she had done to make him run without an explanation.

"For all of that and more," he said.

That was his idea of an apology? She should have known. He'd never been one to open up about his feelings, but she'd hoped that was only age and that maturing would change that side of him. Evidently, it hadn't. "Fine, you said your apology. Now you can go." She forced a smile and waved to Carter, who had climbed up the large slide and was now hollering and waving his arms at her proudly.

Emmitt turned to look at Carter. His eyes widened as he seemed to realize who the boy was for the first time. "He's your son?"

"Yeah, he is. Carter." Mia bit her lip to keep from spilling more. She'd decided on her story over five years ago, and there was no reason to change it now. "After you left, I was a mess, but thankfully Marcus came along and helped me rebuild my life."

"And where is Marcus now?" Emmitt asked looking around the playground.

"Dead," Mia said in a matter-of-fact tone. "He was killed by a drunk driver a year ago."

Emmitt turned to her and reached out a hand. "Mia, I'm so sorry."

"Don't," she said, shying away from his touch. "You don't get to feel badly for me, and you definitely don't get to console me. You lost that privilege when you left without a word after the draft." Unbidden, the image of their last night together flashed into her mind.

"This is so exciting, Emmitt," she said as they watched the teams on the TV announce who they were choosing.

"It's nerve-wracking," he said as he squeezed her hand.

"What if it's New York or California that takes me? I'll be so far away."

"That won't happen." His mother set down a bowl of popcorn on the table in front of them. "I've prayed that God will keep you close."

"Our next team is the San Antonio Saints. They've been watching quite a few players including weak linebacker Emmitt Brown and safety Jordan Granger," one of the announcers said.

"They could definitely use either of those positions, so let's see who they choose," the other announcer said.

The view on the screen shifted to the owners of the San Antonio Saints and the coach stood. "Our pick is Emmitt Brown from Texas Tech University."

"That's you," Mia squealed and pulled Emmitt in for a hug. "San Antonio isn't that far."

"Yeah," he said, but his voice didn't hold the emotion she expected.

"I didn't know how it would be," he said, "and when I got there, it wasn't the life I wanted for you. I wanted you to be able to finish school and go into design, not be my shadow."

"You shouldn't have chosen for me. You never even gave me the option."

"I know. I should have." His gaze dropped to his lap and he ran his thumbs over his forefingers.

"I've thought about that day a lot since I left—"

"But not enough to come back," she said, interrupting him. "You never came home after that. Not even for your family. And I heard they moved a few years ago. Did you do that too? Move them away, so you'd have even less reason to return home and possibly see me?"

He shook his head, but she could see that he knew she was right. It was written all over the expression on his face. "I was selfish then, but I've changed. I became a Christ follower—"

She held up a hand, interrupting him again. "You were already a Christian."

His eyes slowly met hers again, and the sadness in them pulled at her heart. "No, I thought I was, but if I had been, if I'd truly been listening to God, I wouldn't have let that night happen. I took something from you that I shouldn't have— that wasn't mine."

So now he was going to try and be noble? Where had that nobility been for the last five and a half years? "You didn't take it from me. I gave it to you. It takes two, remember?"

"Yes, but had I been the man of God I claimed to be, I wouldn't have let you."

"So, because of that, you thought it would just be better to leave? To never explain yourself? To leave me wondering?" She'd worked so hard to build up her emotional wall, to put him securely behind it at a distance where he could never hurt her again. Yet, sitting here with him, she could feel him chipping away at the wall, and she worked harder to keep it intact.

He opened his mouth to speak, but before he could, a sharp scream followed by loud cries filled the air. Mia bolted toward the playground, screaming Carter's name as she did.

EMMITT WATCHED Mia run toward her son for just a moment before adrenaline kicked in and he followed. A young boy lay on the ground, tears streaming from his face, and his ankle twisted in a painful position.

"It's okay, honey," Mia said, though Emmitt could hear the fear in her voice.

"It hurts Mommy."

"May I?" Emmitt stepped forward and before Mia could object, he lifted the small child in his arms. He looked down at the boy's face and was surprised to see not the blue of Mia's eyes, but dark brown like his. The boy had the same shape to his face as Mia did, and his nose appeared similar, but that's where it ended. The rest of the boy's face must be his father's. Emmitt forced his face to remain stoic as thoughts of a child with Mia surfaced in his mind.

"What are you doing?" Mia asked, following behind him.

"Taking him to the hospital. My car is parked right over there. Did you drive?"

"No, but..."

He could see the hesitation in her face, hear it in her voice. She didn't trust him, which made sense after how he had hurt her, but he was not going to just let this kid keep crying in pain. "Look, I get it. You don't trust me anymore, but I'm here, I have a car, and I can get him there faster than an ambulance could get here. Cheaper too." It was a cheap shot, and he knew it. He could tell money was on her mind more often than it should be, but it worked. Her mouth folded into a tight line, and she nodded.

When they got to his car, he debated his next course of action. His keys were in his pocket, but he would need to set the boy down to get them.

"Where are your keys?" she asked, as if reading his mind.

"In my right front pocket." He indicated with his head and watched as indecision crossed her face. "I can put him down."

"No, I want to move him as little as possible. I'll get them." She took a step closer and then reached into his pocket. Her eyes caught his and a pink flush crawled up her neck. So, he could still affect her. He found that thought satisfying as she certainly still affected him. "Got them," she said and broke their gaze. She unlocked the door and opened it, and Emmitt leaned down and loaded the kid as gently into the backseat as he could.

He moved to shut the door, but she stepped forward. "I'll sit in the back with him."

With a nod, he moved to the driver's side, fired up the car, and pulled out as soon as she was situated.

CHAPTER FIVE

MIA CHEWED on her thumbnail as she paced the hospital restlessly. They had taken Carter for x-rays, but that was nearly an hour ago. Why wasn't he back yet?

"Can I get you anything? A coffee? Food?"

She looked over at Emmitt, who was still waiting with her. She wasn't sure why he hadn't left, but for the moment she was grateful for the company. "No, my stomach is too knotted for anything. What's taking them so long?"

Emmitt shrugged. "I don't know. I'll go ask at the desk."

As he sauntered toward the nurse's station, she resumed her pacing. Suddenly, the doctor who had whisked her son away appeared in the hallway. His grim expression turned her heart to ice. Was it worse than a break?

"Mrs. Conrad, I have some news. Would you like to wait

for your husband to return first?" He nodded toward Emmitt who was returning their direction.

"No, he's not my husband. Just a...a friend." Actually, she didn't know what Emmitt was at the moment, but having driven her here, she supposed he counted as a friend for now.

"All right. Well, Carter did sustain a fracture of his ankle. We got the bone set and the cast on. He'll be groggy for a few hours, but you should be able to take him home tomorrow."

Relief flooded Mia and her shoulders relaxed. "Thank you," she said and then his words registered. "Tomorrow? Is that normal for a break?"

The doctor's lips pursed, and his gaze shifted to the floor before returning to her eyes. "No, it isn't. Unfortunately, we did find something troubling on the x-ray."

"What?" Mia felt as if someone had punched her gut. All the air flew out of her lungs. Her knees buckled and she grabbed for the wall to keep herself from falling.

"There are some markers that indicate osteosarcoma. We'd like to run further tests."

"What is osteosarcoma?" Emmitt asked, coming up beside her. He placed a hand on her shoulder, offering strength. Only a hand, but it was something.

The doctor looked to Mia for consent before answering the question. She hesitated only a moment. If it was something serious, she would have to tell him eventually. "It's fine. He can hear. What is osteosarcoma?"

"It's a cancer of the bone. Has Carter ever complained of his legs hurting before?"

It was Mia's worst nightmare come true, and a weight pressed on her chest, causing her voice to come out small and weak. "Yes, but I thought it was just growing pains." She covered her mouth with her hand. She was an awful mother.

The doctor nodded. "Yes, that's common with this cancer. This type of cancer is usually only found when someone comes in for another type of treatment like Carter's break, and it's rather rare for someone so young, so it's possible it's something else entirely. However, we'd like to be sure, so we'll do a biopsy to determine if it's cancer, and *if* it is, we'll run an MRI to make sure the cancer hasn't spread. Once we know what we're dealing with, we can determine treatment options."

Mia wrung her hands together. Cancer. Was this her fault? Had she passed this to him? Had his father? "Is there something I could have done? If I brought him in sooner?"

"Not necessarily. We won't know exactly what we're dealing with until we run the tests."

Mia nodded, but it didn't ease the guilt that covered her like a second skin. Her voice was barely more than a whisper when she spoke again. "Of course I'll do whatever it takes, but that sounds expensive." The words came out slowly and she hated that instead of just focusing on her son, she was having to think about how she would pay for tests and treatment.

The doctor's face folded in sympathy. "It can get expensive. Do you have insurance?"

Mia shook her head and tried not to feel like a total failure. "My husband died last year, and I've been working at a restaurant. They don't offer insurance."

Pity—that dreaded expression that Mia hated—crossed the doctor's face. "We can work out a payment plan, but we can't move forward until we know what's going on, so not performing the biopsy really isn't an option."

"Of course, I'll figure something out." She didn't know what, as she had no money. Even a payment plan wouldn't help unless they would take twenty dollars a month. She could move out of the apartment, but then where would they live? Back with her parents was possibly an option. One she hated, but what choice did she have? "Can I see Carter?"

"Sure, I'll take you back." The doctor paused and shifted his gaze to Emmitt as if asking silently if he was coming too.

"Go ahead," Emmitt said. "I'll wait for you here and drive you home when you're done."

"You don't have to do that," Mia said. She didn't really want him to stay, but she couldn't just tell him to leave. Not after he'd driven them here and offered to wait around and drive her back. Whatever he had done in the past, he was offering to be her rock right now. And she needed a rock. She hated that she did, but she did.

"I have nothing else to do, remember? I only came here to see you. You go be with your son for as long as you need. I'll be here when you need me."

Mia smiled gratefully and then sighed. Work. She still had to go to work today, but how could she go? Carter needed to stay overnight, and he was too young to stay in the hospital by himself. But, if she didn't go, she would no doubt be fired, and Heaven knew she couldn't afford to take the day off. Especially now. She'd been late too often recently, and her boss would likely not see this as a viable excuse. She'd have to call her mother and see if she could come up to sit with him while she was at work. "Thank you. I won't be long. Unfortunately, I have to be at work in a few hours."

EMMITT WATCHED Mia walk down the hallway and disappear into a room before he returned to the nurses' station. There was no way he was going to let the hospital bills drain Mia financially. The pain and uncertainty had been written all over her face, and her admission that she had no insurance only drove the knife in deeper. If Emmitt had taken Mia with him, if he had married her, she would have insurance.

"Excuse me," he said to the woman at the station, "who do I talk to about paying someone's medical costs?"

The woman smiled at him, but questions swam in her eyes. "I'm sorry? You want to do what?"

"I want to pay for Carter..." He trailed off. He didn't even know Mia's last name. "That woman I was with. Her name is Mia. Her son is young, four or five. He broke his ankle, and I want to pay for his treatment. All of it. His mother doesn't have insurance. Nor does she have the means to pay his bills. I do. So, how do I set that up?"

The woman blinked at him, seemingly incapable of speaking for a minute. "Um, I'll send you to billing. I think they can help you with that, but you'll need his last name."

"Can you help me with that? Please? I don't want to bother his mother while she sits with him, and I'd really like to get this taken care of before she finds out."

The woman bit her lip. "I'm not supposed to."

He was going to have to try a different tactic. He leaned forward and stared directly into her eyes. "What's your name?"

"Betty," she said.

"Well, Betty, do you like football?"

A small smile pulled at the corners of her lips. "This is Texas, sir, it's pretty hard not to like football."

He returned the smile, flashing the most charming one he could. "Okay, well, I play for the San Antonio Saints. I'll send tickets for you and your family back here if you'll help me out."

Her eyes widened as recognition dawned on her face. "You're Emmitt Brown?"

"Yes, I am, and I could use a favor."

She nodded, still apparently awestruck, but her eyes glanced down to the computer screen and her fingers tapped the buttons. "Conrad. His name is Carter Conrad."

"Thank you, Betty." He tapped the counter and then followed her directions down the hall to the billing department where he received the same shocked expression from the woman there.

"Why would you want to pay someone's medical bills?" the woman asked as she pushed dark-rimmed glasses up her nose.

"Because she can't. Because he's a kid." Because it's my fault, he added silently, but this woman didn't need to know that.

"Okay, well, we certainly don't get requests like this every day, but yes, it's possible. I'll have all bills go to your address. I just need you to fill out this form." She slid a paper across the counter to him and Emmitt began filling it out.

"Can you do one more thing?" he asked when he was finished. "Can you make it anonymous?"

"You don't want her to know?"

"Not yet. I'll tell her when it's time."

The woman blinked at him. Clearly this was not normal behavior. "Okay, I'll notate the account."

With that done, Emmitt returned to the waiting area and sat down in one of the chairs. He closed his eyes and placed his chin on his clasped hands. *Lord, I know that doesn't make up for what I've done, but please... If it's Your will, save this boy.*

CHAPTER SIX

MIA TRIED to keep her emotions in check as she entered Carter's room. How could she leave him here to go to work? He looked even smaller than his almost five years in the large bed, especially with the cast dwarfing his ankle. "Hey bud, how are you feeling?"

"Okay," he said with a shrug. "It doesn't hurt so bad anymore and they have TV. Can I stay here for a little bit?"

Mia bit back the tears that threatened to overflow. She should be here with her child all day, but there was little money as it was. That detail was punctuated by the fact that he wanted to stay in a hospital for the TV. What kid wanted to stay in a hospital? Hers, it appeared. Cable had been one of the first things she had dropped after Marcus's death. She had no time to watch it, and the hundred dollars a month was definitely spent better elsewhere. Unfortunately, that meant Carter was reduced to the few DVDs they had purchased over the years if he wanted to watch TV, and Mia knew he was tired of watching the same movies over and over again. Not even the local channels came through their older model television. "Yeah bud. You actually get to spend the night. They want to run some tests on your leg."

"Does that mean I won't have to go to Grandma's?"

"It does, but I still have to go to work, so Grandma will come here. At least until I get off. Then I can come stay with you."

Carter's face scrunched for a moment as if considering this option. "Okay, I think that will be fine. I'm sure I can find some cartoons until Grandma gets here."

Oh, to be a child again and simply worry about cartoons instead of payment plans and treatment options. "That's good, buddy," Mia said as she brushed his bangs back on his forehead. If only it were that simple. She tried not to worry about the future as she looked at him, but it was impossible. How was she ever going to get the money to pay for this stay? Let alone any future tests and treatments he might require? She swallowed the lump forming in her throat and tried to keep her voice even. "I'm going to call Grandma and then I have to get to work, bud, but I'll see you as soon as I get off."

"Okay, bye Mom."

She kissed his forehead and tried to not think about how many more times she would get to do this. What if the cancer was bad? What if he never made it out of this hospital? No, she couldn't think like that. She'd already lost Marcus. She couldn't lose Carter too. That would be too cruel.

As she started back toward the waiting area, the tears built up behind her eyes, blurring her vision, and she sank to the floor. They spilled, one by one, like droplets from a leaky sink down her cheeks, and she pressed her hand to her mouth to keep from crying out. How could this be happening?

"Are you okay?"

Mia looked up to see Emmitt standing over her, concern etched in his handsome features. As he looked down at her, the dam broke. She didn't want his pity, and she lashed out at him.

"No, I'm not okay. My son might have cancer, I have no money to pay for his treatment, and I have to get to work and leave him in the hospital alone. I feel like the worst mother in the world, and you showing up unannounced isn't helping." Her hand flew to her mouth as his face fell. "I'm sorry, that was uncalled for. I know you're just trying to help."

He held out a hand and helped her stand. "It's okay. That's a lot for anyone to deal with, but I'd like to help. Please, tell me what I can do."

Mia blew out a breath that landed somewhere between a chuckle and a sigh and ran her hand through her hair. "Can you cure cancer? Buy me a winning lottery ticket to afford the treatments?" She shook her head and sighed. "I'm sorry, you don't need to be dragged into this. If you can just take me home, you can get back to your life. I'll figure something out."

"How about this? I take you home and then I come back here and hang out with Carter?"

"No, it's fine. I'll call my mother. She usually watches him during the day, so I'm sure she can come in and sit with him."

"Fine, then at least let me buy you dinner tonight."

She started to shake her head again, but he cut her off. "You have to eat, and I'm sure whatever I bring will taste better than hospital food."

"I can just bring something from Manny's," she said. While having company sounded appealing, it was Emmitt. Emmitt, who had always sent her heart fluttering and held a power over her. Emmitt, who had left her with a broken heart. The last thing she needed was to be around Emmitt, especially when she was vulnerable like this.

"I'm not taking no for an answer. I've haven't been the best friend, but friends help each other out."

At the mention of the word friend, she folded. They weren't friends now, but they had been once and though she didn't like asking for help, she didn't have a ton of close friends who could take the time off to sit with her like he could. "Fine, thank you, but I don't get off till nine."

"You're welcome, and that's fine. Now, let's get you home before you're late for another shift."

EMMITT STARED at the open Bible in front of him. He had returned to the hotel room hoping to do his devotional after dropping Mia off at her house, but all he could think about was Carter. Nobody should get cancer, least of all a child with his whole future ahead of him, but Emmitt knew it happened all the time. It had just never happened to someone he knew, and though he didn't have children himself, he couldn't even imagine how Mia must be feeling. He had lifted the financial burden from her shoulders, but he wanted to do more. He just wasn't sure what.

Beside him, his cell phone rang, and he picked it up without even checking the caller ID. "Hello?"

"Rev? It's Tucker Jackson. I need some advice." Tucker was one of the younger players on the team. Picked up in the final round of drafts, he had yet to play a game this season and Emmitt knew he was frustrated by that.

"Sure, Tucker, what can I do for you?" His mind was not really in the right place to be doling out advice, but it was one of the consequences for the character he had created. The men thought because of his faith that he was a good sounding board and they often brought their problems to him. Sometimes he felt more like a Catholic priest than a linebacker.

"I just got word they want to trade me. I don't know what to do, man."

Emmitt's heart hurt for the younger man. It was hard to get on a team, think you were a part of their family, and then realize you didn't mean as much to them as you thought. But being traded also wasn't the worst thing in the world. Yes, he would have to start over on a new team, make new friends, but perhaps he would get to play instead of warming the bench.

"Tucker, I'm sorry. Where do they want to send you, do you know?"

"The Texas Tornadoes. They're a good team, but I feel like I just haven't gotten the chance to show the Saints what I have."

"I know it's hard, but trades are a part of the game. When is the trade happening?"

"As soon as the season is over. The Tornadoes are out of the championship running this season, so they agreed to let me finish the season with the Saints."

Emmitt nodded even though he knew Tucker couldn't see it. Trades were common this time of year. As soon as teams realized they were out of the playoffs, they started looking at how to improve their team for the next year before the draft. Drafts were a crap shoot—owners never really knew what they were getting because college ball was different than pro football. A lot of amazing college players froze when they got out under the cameras. Trades, however, worked more in the owner's favor. They could generally see the player in action in at least one game. Plus, they could put the players through a few extra trainings before the season ended. Emmitt would be sad to see Tucker go, but he couldn't help wondering if they were trading him for a replacement for Matt Johnson. He'd said more than once this was his last year, and the defensive line would crumble without a decent replacement.

"My suggestion is to look at this like an opportunity. You have the chance to show this new team what you have, to show them you belong on the field and not on the bench. I know it's hard to start over, but sometimes it's for the best. And I'll still be here for you. Whatever you need, you can always call on me."

"Thanks, Rev. I think you're what I'm going to miss most. You always made me feel included. Thanks for listening, and I'll see you at practice in a few days."

As Emmitt hung up the phone, Tucker's words raced around in his head. He might have made Tucker feel included, but he'd excluded Mia when it really mattered. He'd left without a word. Embarrassed and ashamed, he hadn't known how to apologize to her, so he'd put it off and thrown himself into playing. And somehow, the days had turned into months and the months into years. And now she was here. Working a dead-end job with little money. And her son was growing up without a father and might have cancer. How costly one choice could be.

Emmitt didn't know what the solution was, but he was determined to make it up to Mia and Carter. Maybe he could become like a surrogate father—one who took the kid to ball games and threw the football around with him. At least that way, he would have a man in his life. Emmitt might have made some huge mistakes in his past, but he was determined to be a good example for the kid. And for Mia. He had to prove to her he had changed.

CHAPTER SEVEN

MIA DID her best to focus on work, but her mind continued to wander to Carter. Was he okay? Lonely? Missing her? She knew her mother was at the hospital with him, but it didn't ease her worry. She should be with him. She should be holding him and spending every second with him. Especially if his seconds were now limited.

"Mia, I need to talk to you," Daryl said, bringing her crashing back to reality.

Her heart sank as she looked at him. His face was long and his bottom lip folded in as if he'd rather be doing anything other than talking to her. And she knew this was it. He was going to fire her. She'd known it would be coming. It wasn't like she could hide her tardiness forever, but she needed this job. Especially now. How would she pay bills if she had no income coming in?

With a heavy heart and an invisible weight pressing down on her shoulders, she followed him to his small office at the back of the restaurant. He shut the door and cleared his throat. "There's no easy way to say this, so I'm just going to come right out with it." His gaze flicked around the room —the dingy walls, the worn carpet, anywhere but her face. "I hear you were late again yesterday."

She wondered how he found out. Had that customer complained after all? It didn't matter, really. What mattered now was owning up and convincing him she would try harder. "I was, and I'm sorry. I wish I could say it won't happen again, but Carter...he's having a hard time."

Daryl held up his hand. "I understand that. Truly, I do..."

Mia hated it when people said that. Especially people like Daryl. Daryl was twenty-two years old, fresh out of college, and his parents owned the restaurant. He had no idea what it was to lose a spouse or raise a child alone and she doubted he lived paycheck to paycheck.

"But I need someone I can count on," he continued. "Someone who isn't going to keep the customers waiting."

"I understand sir, but Carter broke his ankle this morning and is in the hospital. I didn't even stay with him today. I came in even though I wanted to be with him because I need the job." Mia hated begging, especially to someone younger than she was, but she saw no other option.

"I'm sorry to hear that, but I still have to let you go. You can come in tomorrow to pick up your final paycheck, but today is your last shift."

For the second time that day, tears stung her eyes, but Mia was determined not to cry. Not at work and not in front of Daryl. She would figure something out. She didn't know what, but she trusted that God was faithful and He would provide something.

"Understood. Thank you." She left Daryl's office before the tears could start and hurried into the bathroom. Squeezing her eyes shut, she willed the tears away and then splashed water on her face. She would make it through the rest of this day and be the best waitress possible. Maybe Daryl would see and reconsider but even if he didn't, Mia would know that she had done her best and she could leave with her head high. It might not be much of a victory, but pride was about all she had left at the moment, and she would take it.

When her shift ended that evening, she handed in her name tag and apron to Daryl and walked out without another word. Her tears stayed at bay until she shut her car door, and then they streamed down her cheeks in shiny rivulets faster than she could wipe them away. She didn't try to stop them but let them flow. Better to get them out now than cry at the hospital in front of Carter. He would blame himself if he saw her, and she didn't need that.

He was asleep in the bed when she entered the room, and Mia swallowed her disappointment. Even though it was after nine, she'd hoped he would be awake when she arrived, but the biopsy must have worn him out. She motioned her mother to step into the hallway. She needed to talk to her mother, but the conversation wasn't for little ears who would worry too much, and Carter could be a light sleeper.

"How was he today?" Mia asked as she gathered her courage for the harder topic.

"He was fine. Watched entirely too much television, but what else can a boy do when he's confined to a bed. Do you want to tell me how he broke his ankle?"

Mia could hear the blame in her mother's voice and see it in her scolding gaze. Her mother probably thought she hadn't been watching Carter close enough and maybe she hadn't—what with being distracted by Emmitt. It was certainly a lecture Mia had heard more than once, but she couldn't blame her mother. Like Mia, her mother only wanted what was best for Carter, and Mia wished she could provide for him as her parents had provided for her. But she was only one person trying to do the job of two people.

"He fell at the playground today, but there was nothing I could have done. However, his ankle is the least of my worries."

Her mother folded her arms across her chest. "What do you mean? I'd say a broken ankle on a five-year-old is a pretty big deal."

Mia bit the inside of her lip. She did not want to cry in front of her mother. Not because she didn't think her mother would support her but because she was afraid once she started crying, she might not be able to stop. "Not compared to osteosarcoma which the doctor thinks he might have."

As expected, her mother's eyes widened and her hand flew to her mouth. "Cancer? Is that why they took him for tests today?"

Mia swallowed the massive lump in her throat and blinked against the tears that burned in her eyes. "Yeah, and I was fired today for being late yesterday, so on top of dealing with cancer, I have no idea how I'm supposed to pay for any of this."

Compassion flooded her mother's face. "We'll figure this out somehow. You can move back in with us. We can continue to watch Carter while you find a new job. Goodness knows your father is driving me crazy now that he's retired. Having Carter around all day would be good for us."

A tear sneaked out of her eye and trailed down her cheek. Mia swiped it away. "Where am I going to find a new job, Mom? This is Kempton. We only have, like, one job a year open up, and that's usually only when someone goes off to college or dies. It's December, so college is out of the question and I'm not sure I have time to wait for someone to die."

"Then you'll have to look outside of town. It will make

your commute longer, but if you're staying with us, it won't matter because we can put Carter to bed if necessary."

Though that was an option, it was not one Mia enjoyed, as it would mean even less time with Carter than she had now. "Yeah, maybe. I'm not going to start looking tomorrow though. I'm going to stay home with my son and decide what to do. Thank you for sitting with him today."

"Of course. He is my only grandson, and you know I'd do anything for him. However, if you'd only—"

"Mom, stop it." Mia tried not to grimace at her mother's words. While they sounded innocent enough, disappointment threaded them. Disappointment that Mia hadn't had more children before Marcus died. Disappointment in the fact she had married Marcus in the first place and not someone wealthier. But lack of income hadn't been what killed Marcus.

"I'll call you tomorrow, Mom." Mia gave her mother a hug and watched her walk away before re-entering Carter's room. As he still lay sleeping, she pulled up a chair and sat beside him. Relishing the silence, she closed her eyes and opened her heart to God. She needed a miracle and He was the only one who could supply one.

EMMITT GRABBED the bag of Chinese food from the passenger seat of his car. He hoped Mia still liked Chinese.

He had forgotten to ask, but he'd ordered her sweet and sour chicken and broccoli beef, dishes that she'd loved when they'd been together.

A stop at the visitor's desk yielded him a name tag and clearance to continue down the hall, but he stopped short as he entered Carter's room. The boy was asleep in the bed and beside him, Mia sat in a chair with her eyes closed. Should he wake her or just leave the food and go? It was late, but he didn't want her food to spoil. Before he could decide, her body jerked and her eyes flicked open.

"Emmitt? How long have you been there?" She rubbed her eyes as she sat up straighter.

"I just arrived." He held up the bags. "With dinner."

"Thank you." An audible rumble filled the air, and Mia dropped her eyes in embarrassment. "I guess I am hungry."

Emmitt set the bags on the nearby table and pulled a chair over. He handed her one Styrofoam container and then set the other in front of his place. "How are you doing today?" he asked her as he opened the lid. The sweet, salty smell of chicken and rice floated out to him.

"Don't ask," she said with a shake of her head. "My son is sick and in the hospital, and I got fired."

"What?"

"Yeah. It's been a day to say the least." The sarcasm was clear in her voice and Emmitt's heart went out to her. He may have covered her medical bills, but she would never make it without a job. "Sorry, I'm not great company. Would you be willing to pray for the food?"

"Your company is fine," he assured her. "And I don't mind at all."

She nodded, and Emmitt said grace over their dinner. "So why were you working at a restaurant instead of interior design like you studied in college?" he asked after saying Amen. He speared a piece of steak and pepper and shoved it in his mouth. Mia might have preferred milder Chinese dishes, but he enjoyed a little heat in his.

She moved her rice around with her fork as if deciding what she wanted to say. "Well, after you left, I took some time off college to clear my head. Then I met and married Marcus and then Carter was born. I stayed home with him the first few years, but when Marcus died, I had to get a job, and one that paid. As I'd never finished my design degree, no one would hire me, so I turned to waitressing. The work wasn't hard and the tips paid well, but it's been a challenge trying to deal with Carter. He misses his father, and I've been late more times than I'd like to admit. Today, my boss decided he'd had enough and he fired me."

Emmitt swallowed his food and regarded Mia across the table. "What are you going to do?"

"I have no idea. My mother suggested moving in with her and my dad, but not only do I not want to do that, but I don't think it will really save much money, as I'll have to find a job out of town. However, with no job, I don't really have a lot of options."

Before he had thought the idea all the way through, Emmitt blurted out, "Why don't you come work for me?"

"Doing what?" Mia asked with a raised eyebrow. "You're a pro-football player. I don't think I have any skills that would help you."

"Actually, you do. I've been meaning to redecorate my house, but I've been so busy I haven't hired a designer. If you did it, not only could you get publicity that would land you jobs in the future, but you could stay on-site with Carter. I have a guest house in the back."

"Emmitt, I don't think that's a very good idea."

"It's a perfect idea. He could stay in the house with you while you work. I've got a few more days off before I have to be back for practice. I could keep him entertained when you needed quiet time. Plus, we have a great cancer hospital there. *If* it's cancer, they'll probably refer you there anyway."

He could see the hesitation in her eyes, but he also knew he'd hit a nerve with the hospital. Kempton was not known for its hospital care, and she would want the best care for Carter. "You really have a job for me? This isn't just some ruse to get me to your house, so you can break my heart again, is it?"

Her words pierced his heart, but he knew he deserved them. "I really have a job for you. I know I screwed up badly in the past, but let me do this for you."

Mia bit her bottom lip—a trait he had found endearing when they dated and one that always meant she didn't know what to do. Her eyes flicked from him to her son lying in the bed. With a giant sigh, she nodded. "Okay. *If* it's cancer and they refer me to San Antonio's hospital, then I'll do it."

CHAPTER EIGHT

"YOU'RE TAKING my grandson six hours away from here?" The anger and disbelief was evident both in her mother's voice and the stiff posture of her hands jammed onto her hips.

"Hear her out, Maggie," her father said from the kitchen. He had offered to entertain Carter in the other room while the women talked but apparently he was still listening.

"He's offering me a job, Mother. One that pays well and allows me to spend the days with Carter. Plus, the hospital there is top notch. I met with the doctor earlier and the biopsy confirmed it's osteosarcoma. He's referring us to Methodist Hospital anyway for treatment."

"But six hours away? And right before Christmas?"

Mia shrugged. "Faster if you fly, and we can't wait,

Mom. They want to start treatments right away, and we were lucky enough to get an appointment with one of the doctors there tomorrow."

"And who is this mysterious benefactor anyway who swooped in at just the right moment to offer this job?"

Mia bit the inside of her lip. She didn't really want to tell her mother because even though she'd been a fan of Emmitt's in the beginning, she had turned on him when he left Mia, but she would not lie to her either. "It's Emmitt."

As expected, her mother's eyes widened, and her eyebrow arched in that way Mia had always hated as a child —that way that said she was in trouble. "Emmitt Brown? Mia, what are you thinking?"

"I'm thinking that he has money and that he offered me a job. I'm thinking that Carter is going to need to be at a good hospital to get the treatment he needs, and I'm thinking that this offer will allow me to spend time with him both day and night just in case..." Mia didn't finish the thought, but she didn't have to. The expression on her mother's face showed it was heavy on her mind as well.

"He is going to be fine. Do you hear me?"

Mia sniffed back the tears crowding her throat. "He will because he's going to get amazing treatment in San Antonio. I know you will miss him, but this is what he needs right now. This is what I need right now." Though she wished it had been anyone besides Emmitt who had offered her the job, she would not say no to this gift horse. Not only would the job be enough to help pay his medical bills, but Emmitt was well known. If she did a good job, this opportunity could launch her interior design business, and with Carter starting school next year, she wanted a job that she could do during the day to spend time with him at night.

Her mother tilted her chin up and sniffed. "You're right. Go get our boy the best care he can get. Just be careful with your heart, Mia. I don't want to see it get broken again."

"I will, Mom." Though they didn't hug often, Mia pulled her mother in for one now. She had no idea when she might see her again. No idea how long this job would take and no idea how much treatment Carter would need. She was taking a leap of faith, and while she had no problems trusting God, she still had reservations about trusting Emmitt.

"Hey, bud, give Grandma and Grandpa a hug and a kiss, and then we better hit the road." Emmitt had not only offered to forgo his plane tickets and drive with them back to San Antonio, but he had paid for a moving company to box up their things and ship them there. While Mia had no intention of staying forever, she knew Carter would appreciate having his things there—few as they were—and the doctor had said the treatments could take three or four months.

"Bye Grandma," he said as he hobbled over to where they stood. The doctor had placed a walking cast on his foot because crutches were too unwieldy for most children. Still, the sight of him limping tore at Mia's heartstrings, but she knew there was much worse in his future. She prayed he wouldn't lose his smile or his sweet personality on the arduous road ahead.

With the goodbyes said, she helped Carter into her car and then drove to the hotel where Emmitt was staying. As he had flown in initially, they would be dropping his rental car off in town and then heading to San Antonio in her car. She hoped it would make it. Her car was over ten years old and had some quirks.

The air conditioner only worked sixty percent of the time, not favorable when one lived in the hot, dry belt of Texas. Even in December, the temperature often sat in the mid-sixties and the last few days, it had even hit seventy-five a few days. The radio station seemed to only pick up country music even though there was a pop station in town that should have come in clear. And the gas gauge wasn't always reliable. More than once, she had run out of gas on the road and had to walk to the lone gas station and borrow a can to fill up.

"Did you get everything taken care of?" Emmitt asked as he approached the car.

"I think so. Carter's all set back there with some coloring books, his tablet, and a pillow. The moving company is coming this evening to pack everything up and my mother will supervise. Nothing bad will happen on her watch. I grabbed a few snacks for the trip, but I don't have money for gas."

Emmitt waved his hand. "I'll cover the cost of gas. Consider it part of your moving expense, and we'll talk about the rest of the budget when we get there."

Mia took a deep breath and blew it out. "Okay, then I guess we're ready."

EMMITT PLANNED out the drive back in his head as they drove to the rental car company. He still had so much he wanted to tell Mia, but he doubted she would want to talk about the past with Carter in the back seat. Hopefully, he would find some time alone with her after the boy went to sleep. Getting her to take this job had been a miracle, but he kept praying God would give him more opportunities to show her how he'd changed.

After dropping off the keys and transferring his bags to Mia's car, they were on the road again. "Do you remember when we drove back here one Christmas break and I fell asleep at the wheel?" he asked when the silence pressed in on him and he could take it no longer.

It had been a scary trip to say the least. He'd had a late practice, so he'd asked her to take the first shift of driving so he could sleep, but somehow their wires had gotten crossed as she'd had to stay up late for a final. Emmitt had thought he was in better shape than she was, but two hours outside of Lubbock, he'd been woken by the shaking of the car as it swerved over the rumble strips. His eyes had snapped open and his foot had slammed on the brakes as the car fishtailed off the road and into the ditch. Thankfully, the car hadn't been damaged and they'd gotten back on the road ten minutes later. It had taken a lot longer for his heart to slow down.

"Let's not talk about the past," Mia said. "Tell me about football. What's it like?"

Emmitt swallowed his disappointment at her subject change, but he humored her. "It's a lot of work. Four-hour long practices nearly every day except for the days we play or the days we travel. Then there's a lot of soaking sore muscles after and being stretched by the trainer. And don't get me started on ice baths."

"What's an ice bath?" Carter spoke up from the back seat.

Emmitt turned in the seat to look at Carter. The kid was sprawled across the back seat with his foot propped up on a pillow behind Emmitt and his head and back propped against the door behind Mia. His tablet was in his lap, but he was also surrounded by a dozen stuffed animals ranging from dinosaurs to bears, and a stack of books. Did kids always travel with this much stuff?

"An ice bath is just what it sounds like. They fill up a tub with water and ice cubes and then you soak in it.

Supposedly it helps fight tears in muscle fibers and lessens muscle soreness. Some even say it leads to a faster recovery, which I guess I can agree with because I always feel fully recovered after about ten minutes in one of those baths."

Carter grinned at him. "That sounds fun. Do you think it would work for my foot?"

"Ah, I wish, but breaks are a different ball game altogether. Those just take time, my man."

Carter's grin faltered, and his eyes fell to his foot. "Have you ever broken anything, Mr. Brown?"

The kid didn't even know what a loaded question he had asked. Emmitt supposed he had broken Mia's heart and his own for that matter, but as for broken bones... "Just my knuckle when I was young. Before I started playing football, I thought I might like baseball. My first day at tryouts they put me at second base. The ball took a wicked bounce as it reached me, and instead of bouncing into my glove, it hit my ring finger on the other hand. Chipped my knuckle. I kept playing but by the end of the practice, I knew something was wrong because my knuckle had swelled up and was purple."

"I never heard that story," Mia said as she shot him a sideways glance.

Emmitt shrugged. "You never asked about broken bones." In fact, Mia had never asked about his past much at all. He wasn't sure if it was because she genuinely didn't care or because she had worried about him getting injured and hadn't wanted to know.

"Anyway, that's most of my time during the season anyway. Of course, game days are a little different. All the lights and TV crews make it feel surreal, and a lot of times, I'll get done with a game and not even remember what happened. It's like adrenaline kicks in and takes over. I'll watch the game on TV later and it will feel like a whole new game."

"Do you have any off time?" Mia asked.

"Not much during the season. We're on a short break right now so we can celebrate Christmas with our families early. We play on Christmas Eve this year."

She took her eyes off the road long enough to shoot him a wide-eyed gape. "You play on Christmas Eve?"

"Not every year, but this one, yeah, and the rest of this season will be a little tougher because our owner's wife died last week."

Mia shot him another expression that bordered between sympathy and a warning. He realized too late she probably didn't want him talking about death in front of Carter.

"How did she die?" Carter asked from the backseat.

"Old age," Emmitt lied. Though he prided himself on not lying, he thought God would forgive him this one.

"Oh, my dad is in Heaven too. Maybe he'll see your owner's wife."

"Maybe so, kid. Maybe so." Emmitt sat back against the

seat. He'd thought the silence was bad, but having to think about what he said so as not to affect Carter was a lot harder. How did Mia seem to do it so effortlessly?

He sneaked a glance at her from the corner of his eye. Her jaw was tight and her hands clenched the steering wheel, but he'd seen her softer side, and he marveled at how easily she could shift between them. Was that something she'd always been able to do or was that a trait she'd gained with motherhood? He realized he didn't know, and the weight settled on him again. He had been so selfish. How much else had he not noticed about Mia back then?

CHAPTER NINE

"THIS IS WHERE YOU LIVE?" Carter asked in an awed voice as they pulled into the driveway of Emmitt's expansive home.

"It is." He said it matter-of-factly and Mia sensed no bragging or pride in his voice even though the house was clearly worth bragging about. At two stories, it appeared to span half a city block and had to have over three thousand square feet.

"Whoa, and we get to stay here?"

"Well, you can hang out with me during the day while your mom works, but I have a guest house out back that you'll sleep in."

"Why do we have to sleep out back? This place must have like one hundred rooms."

Mia exchanged a quick glance with Emmitt before

answering. He was clearly leaving this up to her to explain. "It just wouldn't be proper for me to stay in a house with Emmitt since we aren't married. It might give people the wrong idea."

"That's stupid," Carter said crossing his arms. "People should mind their own business. Isn't that what you always say, Mom?"

Mia shook her head. Of all the things she said, *that* he decided to listen to. "They should, Carter, but Emmitt is a pro football player and unfortunately that means he is in the public eye more than most people. It's just better this way, and I'm sure the guest house is lovely."

"I think you'll find it suitable," Emmitt said with a laugh. "Shall we head inside and I'll give you the tour?"

Mia agreed, and after helping Carter out of the car, she followed Emmitt up the walkway. Colorful cobbled stones and not concrete made up the path, creating a piece of art work that accented the beautiful shrubbery and flowers along the sides. He must have a gardener and spend a fortune on water because Texas wasn't known for its life-giving rains. Not even in San Antonio.

The expansive front door opened into a large atrium, and her eyes widened as Carter's mouth dropped and "holy cow" slipped out.

"Are you wanting the whole house redesigned?" Mia asked softly. From what she could see, it didn't need it. The house appeared elegantly designed as it was.

"Oh no, not the whole house. Just my bedroom and the family room. The rest of the house was done before I bought it, but I finished the family room after, and I never liked the way the master bedroom was done. The carpet is green, for goodness sake. Who has green carpet?"

Mia had seen several houses with green carpet when she was studying design, but it wasn't her favorite either, and it had to be done with just the right touches or it did look odd.

"Shall I give you the tour and then show you to the guest house?"

Mia and Carter nodded, but neither of them could manage much more than that. His atrium was nearly larger than their whole apartment back in Kempton.

"Okay, well over here is the kitchen."

Kitchen was an understatement. A large island sat in the middle of the room, the gold that threaded the marble gleaming under the bright lights. The double fridge took up half of one wall, and the four ovens took up the rest. There was a large closet-sized pantry and another counter that ran around the rest of the room and under an impressive window. Mia wasn't much of a cook, mainly because she didn't have time, but she thought she might enjoy cooking in a place like this.

The dining room came next, a formal affair with wainscoting and a table that could easily seat twelve. Mia wondered if there was a less formal room to eat in because she could see Carter making a mess of this one.

Emmitt led them to the living room next and Mia nearly echoed the "wow" that came out of Carter's mouth. The far wall not only held a giant big screen television but at least four different gaming devices and a shelving unit full of books, movies, and games.

"Do you know how to play all those?" Carter asked.

Emmitt smiled. "I do, and if it's okay with your mom, we'll play some while she works."

"Please Mom, can we?" Carter turned his puppy dog eyes on Mia, and she sighed. How could she deny him? With his broken foot, it wasn't like he was super mobile anyway, and the time spent here would be something he could remember forever.

"Yes, in moderation. I will not have you playing video games all day."

"Scouts honor," Emmitt said as he held up three fingers. "We'll read and play outside as well."

"Hard to play outside with a cast," Carter grumbled.

"Don't worry, I have ideas."

As Emmitt shot Carter a wink, Mia felt a chink enter her carefully constructed wall. She'd always thought Emmitt would make a wonderful father, and she was getting to see that side of him now. Even more importantly, she was seeing a genuine smile on Carter's face for the first time in a long time. She hoped this hadn't been a terrible idea. She didn't need Carter getting attached to Emmitt. He had made it clear that football meant more to him than anything else.

Finally, they reached the family room. Though built well, Mia could see the tiny clues that it had been added after, and Emmitt hadn't done much with it. The walls were a blank slate, as was the bland furniture.

"What do you want done in here?"

Emmitt shrugged. "I don't really know. I want it to be inviting, a place where people could gather to talk or play games. No TV in here though."

"That sounds lovely," Mia said, but she wondered who the people were. Teammates? A girlfriend? He hadn't mentioned one, but he was too handsome not to have one.

"Yeah, I've always loved the thought of a place where you could unplug from technology and hang out with the people you care most about." His eyes fixed on hers and Mia felt her breath catch. Yes, this had definitely been a terrible idea. Too many more days of him talking like that and looking at her like that and she just might find herself falling for him again. And that would be bad. Very, very bad. Because she was only here for her son. Here to do a job to pay for his bills and here to get him the best care she could. Right?

EMMITT ENJOYED WATCHING the pink tint color Mia's face

and her eyes flick away from his. It meant he still affected her, and if he still affected her then maybe he could have a second chance with her. He hadn't even known he wanted one when he'd made the trip initially to Kempton, but he felt different when he was around her—happier, freer, more content. Emotions he hadn't realized he'd been missing the last few years. Until now.

Plus there was Carter. Though he'd always hoped to have his own children, Carter appeared to be a cool kid. He reminded Emmitt a lot of himself when he was young, and he wondered what it would be like to have a family sitting up in the box watching him play instead of having no one. His parents had come to a few games, but most of Emmitt's tickets were given out to random fans, and while that was nice, it wasn't the same as having family there.

"I'll show you the bedroom later because it's upstairs, but how about I take you to the guest house now and you two can get settled?"

"That sounds great," Mia said.

Emmitt led the way back to the kitchen and opened the sliding glass door. A large patio with a pool, a grill, and several deck chairs separated the main house from the guest house.

"You have a pool?" Carter asked.

"I do, but I'm afraid swimming is out of the question until you get out of that cast, buddy."

"Aw man."

"That's your guest house?" Mia asked, her view going to the large house beyond the pool.

"Yep. It's a three bedroom, two bath house complete with its own kitchen and laundry room."

"Why do you need two houses?" Carter asked as they made their way around the pool.

"I don't usually, but the guest house came with the main house, and I guess it works out for times like these."

"Why do you need such a big house for just you?"

At that Emmitt had to pause. Why had he bought the large estate? Because he'd hoped to fill it with family one day? He'd like to say that was the reason and it was certainly the one he had used to convince himself to plunk down the money required, but if he were honest, it had probably been more for the image. All the players had nice houses and fancy cars, and Emmitt had succumbed to the trap of vanity as well.

He shook his head. Here he thought he'd become so virtuous, reading his Bible every night and going to church and letting the guys call him Rev, but he had just traded one sin for another. "You know what, bud? I really don't, but the house is paid for, so I guess I'll stay here for a while."

Carter shrugged but said nothing more, and Emmitt opened the door to the guest house. "Luckily, this place is a single story," he said as he ushered them in, "so it should be a little easier for you to get around."

The inside of the guest house was much more modest

but still decorated tastefully. The front door opened to a large open concept living room, dining room, and kitchen. To the left, a hallway led to the bedrooms and the hall bathroom.

"This is where we get to stay?" Carter asked.

"Is it okay?" Emmitt had seen the one-bedroom apartment they had been living in back in Kempton, and he'd thought the guest house would still feel like a vacation home compared to it.

"It's awesome. Can I pick my room, Mom?"

"Sure, go ahead," Mia said.

He hobbled down the hallway and then turned. "Mom, you'll get to have your own room too. You won't have to sleep on the couch anymore."

Emmitt dropped his eyes as he saw the blush rise up Mia's neck. He'd suspected she was sleeping on the couch when he'd realized their apartment was only one-bedroom, but hearing it confirmed spurred his guilt once again. Here he had this grandiose house—two of them—and she was sleeping on the couch in her living room.

"Mia, I'm..."

"Don't," she said, cutting him off and shaking her head. Her voice was heavy with emotion. "You made your choice a long time ago, and I made mine. Just because I didn't end up where I'd hoped doesn't mean I want you feeling sorry for me."

No, she never had wanted anyone feeling sorry for her.

She had always been one to see the glass half full, and she had always believed she would do something great with her life. Those were just some of the things he had loved about Mia, so why had he left her? Had he been so scared she wouldn't fit in with his new life? Had he been ashamed of what the other players might think? Mia wasn't classically beautiful, especially with her face full of freckles. She was more girl next door than runway model, but she had always been beautiful to him.

Or had he really just been running from their night together? Even though they'd planned to wait until marriage, he had slipped the night of the draft pick. He'd been so excited and he'd wanted to share that excitement with her. He'd wanted to share everything with her, and it had been an amazing night. Until the reality of it crept in. Until he began to worry about the disappointment both their families would feel if they found out. Until the thought of running away to escape the shame convinced him to leave the one thing that had truly made him happy. Until the guilt had taken ahold of him, tied a noose around his neck, and told him he was no longer good enough for her.

"Why don't you go check out the master suite while I go get the luggage?" he said, changing the subject. The guilt lay heavy in the air tonight, and he could feel Satan trying to grab control of him, trying to whisper how awful he had been to leave Mia without a word, and how he deserved the single life he had chosen.

He stepped outside and let the cool air wash over him. He'd fought those feelings for so long, and he'd made peace with God, but making peace with Mia was a whole new thing. It was harder, especially with everything life had thrown at her. He touched the small gold cross that hung around his neck as a reminder and turned his face toward the sky. "Lord, help me to show her I've changed and help me help her."

CHAPTER TEN

MIA AWOKE with a start and looked around the unfamiliar room a moment before reality came crashing back in on her. She was in Emmitt's guest house. She was going to decorate two rooms in his house. Her son had cancer. Those last four words were sobering enough to wake her completely and urge her to tiptoe in to check on Carter.

He had chosen the room next to hers, and she was glad. She'd always been protective of him, but now she felt the need to watch him constantly, which was irrational. The doctor had been optimistic when he told her the tumor was in Carter's bone and would require chemo and surgery, but he felt the prognosis was good. And it wasn't like Carter had succumbed to brittle bone disease all of a sudden. He wasn't more likely to break any more bones than he would have been a year ago, but knowing that didn't stop the fear from creeping up her throat.

She pushed open his door. Just to make sure he didn't need anything, she told herself, but it was really to verify that his chest still rose and fell. That oxygen still filled his lungs. That he hadn't passed away in the night. It was morbid, she knew, but that's what the word cancer did. It left black clouds of questions and doubts and fears hanging in the air. Clouds that followed her wherever she went.

Carter lay in the large bed, his dinosaur pajama-clad arms peeking out from under the covers. She held her breath and watched, but yes, the blanket rose and fell with his rhythmic breathing. Relief flooded her. She could relax a little, long enough to take a shower at least. And maybe have some breakfast.

She had just sat down with her Bible and a cup of coffee when the soft thumps of Carter's walking cast carried down the hall.

"Hey bud, how did you sleep?" she asked when he reached the kitchen.

"Mostly good. I miss the rest of my stuffies, but they'll be here soon, right?"

A smile pulled at the corners of Mia's lips. Even with everything going on with him, all he could think about was his stuffed animals. "Yes, bud. The movers should arrive today and then all your stuff will be here."

"Cool. What's for breakfast?"

Mia nearly laughed out loud at the sudden shift in topic. Carter had always been like that. Once he got the answer to his question, there was no need to discuss it any further. He was ready to move on. "I don't know. Let me look."

She hadn't taken the time last night to peruse the kitchen offerings so she hoped that something lay in the cupboards. They could always walk over to the main house, but that might mean eating with Emmitt, and Mia wanted to avoid that as much as possible. It was hard enough to fight old feelings just being near him and in his guest house, but she knew it would get infinitely harder if she began doing routine things with him like eating meals and watching TV. No, she needed to keep those boundaries up as much as she could. To protect herself. And to protect Carter.

"Let's see. I spy some cereal. If we have milk, are you up for that?"

His face scrunched as he climbed into one of the chairs at the table. "Is there Cinnamon Toast Crunch or something chocolaty?"

"Um..." Mia perused the offerings. Raisin Bran, Cheerios, and... "I think you might be in luck. This looks like Cinnamon Toast Crunch."

"Yes, I'll take it."

Another few minutes of searching yielded a bowl, a spoon, and some fresh milk. As Mia poured Carter's cereal, she wondered if Emmitt kept this place stocked all the time or if he had called ahead and had someone do that for him.

He certainly hadn't had time to stock it himself, but if he did keep it stocked, who usually stayed here? Friends? Family? Women?

She shook her head to clear that thought. There was no need to picture the parade of women that must march through Emmitt's life as a professional athlete. Was that why he had left her? Had he been ashamed of her? Or had he just wanted to be free to date whoever might throw themselves at him? Nope, she didn't need to think about that either. The past was the past, and it needed to stay there. And his present was...well, she didn't know what it was, but what happened in his life now was none of her concern.

Her stomach rumbled, reminding her that she hadn't eaten either, and after the refrigerator yielded fresh eggs and bacon, she fried some up and joined Carter at the table. It would be a long day today. She planned to draw up some designs for Emmitt's family room and bedroom, then she and Carter had a meeting with the cancer treatment team at the Methodist Children's Hospital. Her doctor in Kempton had told her to be ready for chemo treatments anywhere from a month to ten weeks before surgery and then for several treatments after surgery. Mia had no idea if the job for Emmitt would take that long, and she wondered where they would stay if she finished early.

EMMITT WOKE with a smile on his face. He'd enjoyed showing Mia and Carter around his place yesterday, and he was looking forward to spending the day with them. Maybe he would even take them shopping with him. Christmas was only a few days away and his place had no spirit, but for the first time in years, he wanted it to.

After a quick shower, he headed downstairs to see what Anton, his cook and personal assistant, was whipping up for breakfast. Anton was a nutritionist who specialized in athletic fitness. Emmitt had been fortunate enough to find him through one of the coach's referrals, and he'd agreed to take on the role of preparing Emmitt's food and watching the house while he was gone. Anton had quickly become a close friend as well.

The smell of bacon and eggs greeted him as he walked into the kitchen. Anton stood by the stove, a spatula in hand. "You're back early. I wasn't expecting you for a few more days."

Emmitt nodded. "Yes, I was expecting to stay there longer, but it turned out not to be necessary. Did you get the guest house stocked as I asked?" He hoped Anton had picked up the groceries he'd asked him to. It would be awful if Mia woke up to empty cupboards.

"I did. Do you want to tell me who is staying at the guest house?"

"A friend who needed a job and a place to stay close to Methodist Hospital."

Anton's brow shot up as he turned the burner off and filled a plate for Emmitt and one for himself. "Uh huh, and does this friend have a name?" He flashed Emmitt an inquisitive expression as he set the plate in front of him.

"Mia," Emmitt said.

"As in ex-girlfriend Mia?" Anton's eyes widened as he sat down across from Emmitt. He didn't always eat meals with Emmitt but he would when he had time.

"Yes, that's the one. After Diana's death, Matt decided we should live without regrets, so he asked us all to take care of whatever we regretted. The way I left Mia when I joined the Saints is my biggest regret."

"And is she sick?"

"No, her son is. Osteosarcoma."

"Whew." Anton let out a low whistle. "That's heavy. You sure you want to get involved in that?"

Emmitt sighed. "I have to. It's my fault that she didn't become a designer. When I left without an explanation, she took time off college and never returned. I can't make up for the past, but I can help her future. So, I hired her to redo the family room and my bedroom."

Anton looked as if he wanted to say more, but before he could, the sliding glass door opened, and Mia and Carter stepped in.

"Oh, I'm sorry," Mia said when her eyes landed on Anton. "I hope we aren't interrupting anything."

"No, you're fine. Mia, this is my friend and

personal assistant, Anton. Anton, this is Mia and her son, Carter." A feeling of sadness swept across Emmitt as he took in the dark circles under Mia's eyes. He had hoped offering her a job would ease some of her worry, but he should have known better. Cancer was enough to worry anyone, and he couldn't imagine it affecting a child.

Anton swallowed his bite and then stood and held out a hand. "Pleased to meet you, Mia, Carter. I also cook Emmitt's meals, so feel free to join him if you'd like."

"Oh, we're fine. It seems someone stocked the guest house for us. I assume that was you."

"Yes, ma'am," Anton said with a nod. "And if you need anything else, just leave a list on the counter here, and I'll happily pick it up for you."

"Thank you, but I'm sure whatever you bought will be fine." Mia turned her gaze to Emmitt. "When you're done, do you think you could show me the bedroom? I'd like to start working on plans this morning before Carter's appointment."

Right, Carter's appointment. He had forgotten that was today. Well, that might change Emmitt's plans, but perhaps he could drive them and then they could all go shopping after. "Of course." He shoveled the last bite of egg into his mouth and picked up the last strip of bacon. "I'm ready now," he said when he finished chewing.

Mia nodded, but her gaze slipped to Carter.

"I could get Carter set up with a video game if that's all right with you," Anton said.

"Please Mom?" Carter begged.

Mia hesitated a moment before nodding. "Sure, that would be fine. Thank you."

"Yay, what all does he have? Not that it matters. I don't have a game system, so I haven't played much anyway."

Emmitt bit back a smile as Anton led Carter from the room. Then he turned to Mia. "Shall we?"

"Yeah, sure," Mia said, though her gaze remained on the empty doorway her son had passed through.

Emmitt led the way up the stairs and down the short hallway to the master bedroom. As he pushed open the door, he scanned the area quickly. He was rather certain he had put everything away, but it never hurt to double check.

"Ah, I see what you mean," Mia said, stepping into the room. Her eyes scanned the room, and he tried to look at it from a designer's point of view. The furniture was probably fine, but he had done nothing to bring any sort of theme into the room. And it was a large open space with only his bed, nightstand, and dresser filling any of the room.

"Do you have any thoughts for how you want the room to look?"

Emmitt shook his head. Design was definitely not his thing. "Uh, inviting? I want it to be a relaxing space where I can unwind. The only thing I know for sure is no more green carpet. Maybe a beige or tan carpet?"

Mia chuckled and shook her head. "You never were much for the intricacies, were you?"

"I'm not even sure I know what the inter...intra...whatever you said are," he said with a laugh.

"Okay, well I have some ideas. You have a great space here that you could do a lot with. What if we went with neutral tones and added a chest to the foot of the bed to store blankets and things in? Then we could add a chair and a reading lamp to the window. Once it has new curtains, it would be the perfect reading spot. A few landscape pictures would bring the room to life as well. Are you okay if I change your bedding?"

Emmitt smiled as Mia rattled off everything she wanted to do. He didn't know what half of it meant, and he wasn't sure he'd ever use a reading corner, but he could see her curled up there, reading at night while he watched TV. "I'm okay with whatever you want to do. I hired you for your creative eye and mind."

"All right. Well, I'll draw up a few plans to show you and then we can discuss the budget. Sound good?"

"Sounds perfect," Emmitt said with a smile.

CHAPTER ELEVEN

WITH A SIGH, Mia shut off the alarm on her phone and set her pencil down. She hadn't gotten as much done on the designs as she wanted to, but it was time to head to the hospital for Carter's appointment.

She wandered out of the dining room, where she had been working, into the living room. Carter sat on a footstool while Emmitt sat in a chair next to him. Some racing video game was on the screen, but that wasn't what caught her eye. No, what caught her eye was the smile on Carter's face, the light emanating from his eyes that she hadn't seen in a long time, and the matching expression on Emmitt's face. He was like a big kid himself. Always had been.

She'd met him in high school when her family moved to Kempton. Her dad had thought it would be a nice sleepy town to retire in. Mia had thought it was just sleepy, but then she'd met Emmitt, star defensive player for the Kempton Kings, and he had stolen her heart. Well, first he'd stolen her notebook. Then he'd stolen her heart.

Mia had always been a sketcher, and she took her notebook with her everywhere. Emmitt had tried to get her attention, but she'd been too angry at moving to the small town to care about anything, including boys. Then one day her notebook had disappeared. When he returned it later, he had drawn a horrible picture of the two of them with the words 'Will you go out with me?' underneath. Annoyed and flattered at the same time, Mia had agreed, and they'd quickly become inseparable. They'd even attended college together, though Mia had been a year behind him, but when he got drafted everything had changed.

And she would do well to remember that. He might look different now and say the right words, but she was sure he was the same selfish person inside. The person who had spent a night with her and then left without a word. The person who had shattered her heart into a million pieces.

"Carter, buddy, we have to go."

"Aw, Mom, do we have to?"

"Yes, we have to. We have an appointment in an hour and I have no idea how bad the traffic might be." In fact, she didn't even know exactly where she was going. She would be relying on her map app to lead the way. It was usually correct, although once or twice it had led her into a neighborhood when she was looking for a restaurant or vice versa.

Emmitt looked up at her. "How about you let me drive?"

Mia shook her head. "No, that's not necessary. I'm sure I can find it."

"I'm sure you can as well, but I was hoping we could do some Christmas shopping afterwards. This place could use some seasonal cheer."

A smile stretched across Carter's face. "Yeah, Mom, can we? We haven't decorated for Christmas yet and it's only a week away. How will Santa find us if we don't decorate?"

Mia sucked in her breath and bit her lip. She didn't need to spend any more time with Emmitt, but how did she say no to Carter? The answer clearly was that she didn't. Not with everything that was happening to him. "Fine, but only if he isn't too tired afterwards."

"Yay," Carter hollered and the two high-fived. Mia shook her head. She loved seeing her son happy, but she didn't need him getting attached to Emmitt, because eventually they would be going home and he would be staying here. And he'd already broken her heart—she didn't need him breaking her son's as well.

The ride to the hospital wasn't quiet—Emmitt and Carter continued to jabber on about some video game—but Mia was absorbed in her own thoughts. This would be the first time meeting with Carter's new team and she had no idea what to expect.

"Would you like me to come in with you?"

Mia jumped at Emmitt's words and his hand on her

arm. She had planned to say no—she'd lived without him the last five years and she could continue to do so—but going in alone now that they were here felt daunting. "Please." It was only one word, but it was all she could muster. Fear clawed at her throat and pressed against her windpipe.

"Of course." He turned off the car and opened the door for Mia before helping Carter out of the back seat.

As they walked into the hospital, the urge to grab his hand swept over Mia. She wanted the comfort of his touch, but she couldn't do it. Wouldn't do it. Not after the way he'd left.

"I'm Mia Conrad. We have an appointment for Carter Conrad," Mia said when they approached the check-in desk.

The woman smiled at them and then looked up their appointment. "Yes, you're all checked in. Dr. Goodwin will be with you soon."

"Is this going to hurt, Mommy?" Carter asked as they sat down. Mia's heart broke at the fear in his voice, and though she could lie to him, she wasn't going to.

"I don't know, honey, but what I do know is that this will make the pain you've been feeling in your leg stop. That's good, right?"

"Yeah, I guess." But his eyes dropped to the floor.

"Hey, after this, how about you pick out the tree from the lot?" Emmitt asked. "Any tree you want."

Carter glanced up at him. "And decorations?"

"You bet. We have to deck the place out good."

Though Carter perked up a little at that, Mia could still sense the cloud of fear hanging around him, see the weight of it pressing in on his small shoulders. When would they catch a break?

EMMITT COULDN'T IMAGINE the anxiety coursing through Mia, though he could see it on her guarded expression as she stared out the window. Carter wasn't even his kid and he was worried. The doctor had suggested ten weeks of chemotherapy before the surgery to remove the tumor and then another five weeks of chemo after. Plus, there would be the side effects of chemo to deal with—nausea, vomiting, mouth sores. None of it sounded fun to Emmitt, but he was determined to cheer them both up.

He pulled into The Christmas Store, which was a store that specialized in Christmas offerings year-round. Emmitt had no idea how they stayed in business the other ten months of the year, but he was glad they existed today.

"Let's go get a tree," he announced, forcing cheer into his voice. Perhaps if he could fake it enough, it would rub off on all of them.

The somber mood lasted until they stepped inside the building. Then Carter's eyes lit up and the corners of his mouth twitched. "Wow, I've never seen anything like this."

Even Mia appeared speechless as she gazed in wonder

at the store. The front was filled with artificial trees of all kinds. Along the walls were rows and rows of ornaments, and upstairs was filled with trains and miniature villages, stockings, and cards. "This is..."

"Magical, right?" Emmitt smiled at her, remembering their last Christmas together. He'd been so close to buying her a ring that year, but his so-called friends—the other players on his college team—had told him to wait. They had warned him that pro football was different, that he might have to move across the country, that a long-distance relationship would never last, that he didn't want to settle until he knew what was really out there. And he had listened to them. He had let their stupid words fester in his brain until they felt true, and he hadn't bought the ring. Instead he'd bought her a leather-bound sketch book—still something she enjoyed but not the gift he should have given her.

She caught his eye and smiled. It was still guarded, but he wondered if she were remembering past Christmases. Ones when it actually snowed and they chased each other around his yard and built giant snowmen. Others where it was cold but the snow refused to fall and they would sit by his fireplace and stare out the large bay window sipping hot chocolate. He hadn't had a Christmas like that since he left. Now, his Christmases were either a quick trip to Florida where his parents lived or games. He didn't even think he'd put up a tree in the last five years.

"Let's pick a tree first," Carter said, eyeing the forest

before them. He might have had a cast on, but he was still quick when he wanted to be, and he took off down the right side of trees. "I want a giant one," he shouted back to them.

"Thank you for doing this," Mia said as they followed in his wake.

"You're welcome. I only wish I could do more." And then he realized he could. He turned to her and grabbed her hands before he thought about it. "Mia, the guest house is yours for as long as you need it. Even if you finish the job earlier, feel free to stay as long as you need to."

Her eyes caught his and then fell to their clasped hands. "Emmitt, I..."

"No, I'm serious. No one uses the guest house, so it's yours, and it would be cheaper than flying back and forth for treatment."

"Mom, Emmitt, come see this one," Carter called to them, and just like that, the spell was broken.

Mia pulled her hands out of his grip and headed toward Carter. "Thank you, Emmitt. We'll see."

He hated the expression on her face, the distrust she still held for him, though he couldn't blame her. Even more, he hated that he had made her that way, and he wondered if he would ever be able to redeem his actions of five years ago.

CHAPTER TWELVE

MIA WATCHED Emmitt struggle with the enormous tree. She should probably offer to help, but it was much more entertaining watching him wrestle the monstrous beast Carter had picked out. It had to be nearly eight feet tall and at least three feet around. It was a good thing it was an artificial tree because Mia couldn't imagine the cleanup from all those needles had it been a real tree.

"No one help me here," Emmitt teased. "I've got this all under control."

Across the room, Carter giggled from his perch on the couch. Bags of ornaments surrounded him, and he pulled them out one by one and snipped off the tags. "It looks like the tree ate you."

"I hope not," Emmitt said as he pushed the tree into the final position and stepped back. "I don't think I'd taste very good." He plugged in the cord and the lights on the tree came to life.

"It's so pretty," Carter said. "Can we hang the ornaments now?"

"We can, but let's move them a little closer so you don't have to walk so far." Emmitt gathered the bags and placed them closer to the tree and then fished out the package of hooks. "Want to help us, Mia?"

A million reasons as to why she shouldn't flooded her mind. How many times had she done this with Emmitt and imagined their future together? Imagined the sound of Christmas music filling the air and the two of them dancing around the tree in their socks and pajamas. Imagined him lifting their son or daughter up to place the angel on top of the tree. Too many times for sure, but those were different times. Tonight was about making Carter happy, so she agreed.

There was no music playing, but Mia could almost forget about Carter's cancer as she watched him hobble to the tree and hang his ornaments. He had always loved Christmas and loved decorating their much smaller tree at home, but his favorite thing had always been opening gifts. She wondered what she would get him this year as she had no money. Would it be awful if she asked Emmitt for an advance to buy Carter a few gifts? Surely, he would understand the reason for it. She would ask him tonight once Carter was asleep.

It took them nearly an hour but finally the tree was fully decorated, and while it wasn't beautiful in the traditional sense—Carter had a tendency to place a lot of ornaments in the same spot, leaving other large patches bare—it was beautiful to her.

"Want to put the angel on top?" Emmitt asked Carter.

Carter nodded and grabbed the golden angel. "Be careful," Mia said as Emmitt bent to lift him. Though she knew from his well-defined shoulders and biceps that he was probably strong enough, fears of Carter falling and breaking another bone rushed through her mind.

"I'll be careful. I promise," Emmitt said. With ease, he scooped Carter up and held him in place until the angel was situated. Then he returned him to the ground just as softly. It was the perfect picture Mia had always imagined it would be, and it pulled at her heartstrings.

"Okay, buddy, let's get you to bed," Mia said. It wasn't that far past his bedtime, but she needed to break up this family picture before she said something she might regret later.

"Aw, Mom, do I have to?"

"Yes, you have to. I need you to get some good sleep tonight before your first treatment tomorrow."

"Okay," he said with a sigh. "Night, Mr. Emmitt."

"Night, buddy. We'll hang out again tomorrow before your appointment." He ruffled Carter's hair and the boy turned adoring eyes up at him.

Oh, dear. Mia had been hoping not to see this bond develop. Yes, she wanted a man in Carter's life, but she wanted someone he could look up to. Someone who would be around while he was growing up. And that someone was definitely not Emmitt. She should have thought this through better. She should have known that Emmitt, with his charming smile and house of toys, would have been like candy to a kid such as Carter who had none.

"I'm going to put him to bed, but then can we talk for a minute?" Mia asked Emmitt.

"Sure. I'll be in the living room. Join me whenever you're ready."

Mia nodded and escorted Carter out of the main house.

"Mr. Emmitt is awful nice, isn't he, Mom?" Carter asked as they entered his room.

Mia pursed her lips together as she thought about how to answer him. "He is, buddy, but Emmitt's job keeps him busy a lot of the time. In fact, he'll probably have a game coming up soon, so don't be surprised if he isn't around as much when that happens."

The movers had arrived earlier, but they hadn't unpacked the boxes and in all the commotion, Mia had forgotten to do it as well. She opened the boxes and began searching for a pair of jammies for Carter.

"Can we watch him play some time?" Carter asked, stifling a yawn.

"Maybe, but we're not really here to watch Emmitt.

We're here for me to work and you to get better." Nope, this one was more stuffed animals. He would want those tomorrow, but she wouldn't mention them now or he would have a fit searching for every stuffed animal until he found them all.

"But can't we do both?" He sat on the bed and Mia saw the dark circles under his eyes. He needed sleep. She opened the next box. Bingo.

Thankfully, the movers had packed the clothes nicely instead of just throwing them in a box—Mia wondered how much extra Emmitt had paid for that service—and a pair of matching jammies lay right on top. "We'll see, bud," she said as she helped him out of his clothes and into the pajamas.

"I think it would be cool if Mr. Emmitt were my new dad," he said as his head hit the pillow. "Do you think you might ever marry him?"

What did she say to that? Did she tell Carter she had planned to marry Emmitt? That she had thought out their wedding down to the type of cake and the first song they would dance to? That she had imagined herself at every game of his, cheering him on? Of course she didn't. That would be too much for his four-year-old brain to handle. Heck, it was too much for her twenty-five-year-old brain sometimes.

"I think I could marry someone like him," she said instead. "If God sends the right man to me."

Carter's eyes closed and his hand curled under his

pillow. Mia watched him for a moment. In this bed, he didn't look sick. He looked content and happy. If only she could keep him like this forever. His eyes popped open and focused on her. "Maybe He already has," he said sleepily and then his eyes shut again.

Mia waited for him to say more, but the rhythmic rise and fall of his chest told her he had drifted off to dreamland. Was Carter right? Was God giving her and Emmitt another chance? No, this was business and nothing more. She needed to remember that. He was her boss, not her boyfriend, and she was about to ask him for an advance.

EMMITT SAT in the living room waiting for Mia to return. What did she want to talk to him about? Was it possible that she was walking down memory lane like he was? Had she felt the electricity between them earlier as he had? The soft pad of a footfall grabbed his attention, and he looked up to see her in the doorway.

Her face held a conflicted expression, and he wondered what was going on in her head. "Hey, come on in. Do you want anything to drink?"

"No, I'm good," she said, shaking her head. "This won't take long." She crossed the room to the chair across from him and sat down. She folded her hands in her lap and

LORANA HOOPES

stared down at them a moment. "I need to ask you something."

"Sure, anything." He scooted toward the edge of the chair to lean closer to her.

"Well, I know I haven't started yet, but Christmas is less than a week away, and I really want to get Carter something. However, as you know, I have no money. Do you think I could get a small advance? Just enough to buy him a gift?"

Emmitt had not been expecting those words. Nor had he thought about the fact that Mia might not have enough money to buy presents for Carter. It was sobering to say the least. "Yes, of course, and I'd be happy to purchase a few gifts as well." He was already making a list of everything he would love to get the boy.

Mia held up her hand and shook her head. "No, that won't be necessary. Today was great, but I can't let you spoil him. It would make it even worse when we go home and he has to go back to our little house without all of this." She waved her hand around the room.

"What if you don't?" Emmitt asked.

"What if I don't what?" Her eyes locked on his, and Emmitt felt his courage wane. Was this what he wanted? He should be sure before he offered. It wouldn't be fair to do this to her again.

But he was sure. He'd been almost positive when he'd seen her for the first time back in Kempton, and today had solidified that feeling. He wanted Mia back in his life. And

Carter too. He wanted a family. "What if you don't go back?"

He grabbed her hands and stood, pulling her up beside him. "What if you stay? What if we try again? I was wrong to leave last time, Mia. I was weak and confused and I let others' opinions sway my own. But, I've been on my own for the last few years, and I've hated it. Being with you these last few days has made me realize how much I want this. You. Carter. A family. What if God brought us back together so we could have a second chance?"

Something flickered in her eyes. Surprise? Confusion? Joy? He couldn't tell. "Emmitt, I..."

He needed to show her—to convince her that he'd changed. He pulled her closer and lowered his face to kiss her, but before he could, she placed a finger on his lips.

"I don't think it's a good idea, Emmitt. You're my boss right now, and I should focus on that."

Right. Boss. He had thought she was feeling something too, but she was just doing her job. He'd lost his chance with her. He dropped her hands and took a step back. "You're right, of course. I'll be happy to give you an advance of whatever you need."

"Thank you," Mia said. "I'll list what we need to purchase tomorrow so I can get started for you."

Emmitt nodded and watched her walk toward the doorway. "Mia?" She turned and looked at him. "Will you and Carter at least come to my game on Christmas Eve? I have box seats and no one to ever use them. It would mean a lot if you would watch me play."

A small smile pulled at her lips. "We'll see." And then she was gone.

Emmitt sank down into the chair and dropped his head into his hands. Right now, he hated Matt for pushing them to do this 'no regrets' pact. True, he had apologized for his regret, but now he was seeing what he could have had—what he threw away—and realizing that he would never get that. At least not with Mia. And Emmitt thought that that realization might be worse than any regret he might have had. Because this regret would never change.

CHAPTER THIRTEEN

A SIGH ESCAPED Mia's lips as she stared at the list she had created. She needed to unpack their things, purchase the supplies she would need to do the rooms for Emmitt, and take Carter to his appointment that afternoon. It felt like more than she could do in a week, much less a day.

"Can I have cereal again, Mom?"

Mia smiled at Carter, who had hobbled into the kitchen and stood staring at her in his too small train pajamas. Clothes. She needed to buy him clothes as well. "Of course, bud." She took a bowl down from the cupboard and filled it with cereal. "Do you think you could unpack some of your boxes today while I'm working?" she asked as she grabbed the milk from the fridge and filled the bowl.

"By myself?" Carter asked.

"Yes, by yourself. I need to get some work done for Emmitt today, and I won't have time."

"Maybe Mr. Emmitt would help me unpack," Carter said excitedly. "Then we could get done quicker and play games."

"I don't think Mr. Emmitt has time to do that. He has a game he needs to start preparing for." She set the bowl down in front of him and then filled her mug with coffee before sitting down.

"We could at least ask," Carter grumbled as he shoved the spoon into the bowl.

Mia opened her mouth to respond, but before she could, a knock sounded at the door. Emmitt? It had to be as she knew no one else here.

She opened the door to find not only Emmitt but Anton and a pretty brunette.

"Oh, good, I was hoping we wouldn't wake you," Emmitt said. "Can we come in?"

"Um, sure." Mia held the door open and stepped back. What were they doing here and who was the woman? She was glad she had gotten dressed before making her coffee this morning.

"Mr. Emmitt, do you want to help me unpack this morning?" Carter asked.

"Carter," Mia began, but Emmitt cut her off.

"That would be great. How about Mr. Anton and I help

you guys get settled here and Kris here can help your mom with decorating?"

"Hi, I'm Kris with a K. It's short for Kristina," the woman said, stepping forward and holding out her hand. "Also known as Anton's better half."

"Hah, you wish, woman," Anton said with an affectionate smile. It was clear these two were dating.

"Um, nice to meet you," Mia said, returning the shake. "I appreciate the offer, Emmitt, but I should probably unpack myself."

"Nonsense, Mia. You have a lot on your plate already. Let us help you. It's what friends are for."

Mia barely knew Anton and she had just met Kris, but she couldn't deny the help would ease her over-full schedule. "Okay," she agreed with a sigh, "but you can leave the boxes in my room alone. I'll take care of those."

"Deal," Emmitt said.

"And I'd love to offer my help with whatever you need. I'm not a designer, but I've watched a lot of shows on TV and would love to see the action in person," Kris said. "Plus, I know my way around the city if we need to purchase anything."

"We definitely do," Mia said with a small smile before turning her eyes to Emmitt and Anton. "Okay, if you're sure."

"We're sure. We'll have this place all unpacked and set up for you guys before Carter's appointment today."

Mia still wasn't sure this was the best idea. Having Carter spend more time with Emmitt without her would probably just deepen his desire to have the man as a father, but it did appear to be the best option for her to get everything done.

"All right," she said with a sigh and walked back to the table to grab her list. "Kris, do you want to come with me and we'll see what we still need to purchase?"

"You bet. Whatever you need."

Mia turned to Carter. "You be on your best behavior for Mr. Emmitt and Mr. Anton, do you hear?"

"Aw, Mom, I'm not a little kid," he mumbled as pink spread out along his cheeks. But that's exactly what he was. A little kid. Her kid. Hers and Emmitt's.

She glanced up at Emmitt, wondering if he had figured it out yet. Had he processed the timeline? She'd been careful to be vague, and strangely, Carter didn't look much like Emmitt. Not yet anyway, but she could see more of his features appearing in the boy's face every day. His eyes were beginning to take on the same shape as Emmitt's, and a dimple had appeared in his cheek a few months ago. A dimple that looked very much like the one Mia used to tease Emmitt about even though she had always loved it.

She would have to tell Emmitt—but not yet. Not until she was sure. Sure that he wouldn't disappear again and leave them in a lurch like he had last time. True, he hadn't known about the baby and perhaps he would have come back for her if he had, but Mia hadn't wanted that kind of relationship. She wanted to know he *wanted* to be with her, not that he was with her because he felt he had to be. She wanted love and not just a sense of duty.

She shook her head to clear the thoughts. There was no time to think about that now. "Just remember your manners," she said to Carter and then led the way out of the guesthouse.

Emmitt watched Mia exit with Kris before turning to Anton. "You sure it was a good idea to get Kris involved?" He didn't know Kris well, as Anton usually didn't bring her over, but she'd seemed pleasant enough the few times he had met her. Still, he didn't want to overwhelm Mia.

"She wanted to, man. She loves to help. Besides, you want Mia to stay, right?"

Emmitt nodded. More than anything he wanted Mia and Carter to stay.

"Then she needs a friend here. If there's one thing I've learned about women, it's that they need someone to vent to. Kris is great at listening."

"Are we staying?" Carter asked. "Like forever?"

Anton blanched as Emmitt turned to Carter. He hadn't thought the boy had been listening. "Would you like that?"

The smile that lit up Carter's face stretched from ear to

ear. "I'd love that," he shouted. "I told Momma last night that you should be my new dad."

Emmitt blinked, shocked at the kid's honesty. "Oh, and what did your mom say to that?"

"She said she'd marry someone like you. If God sent her the right man, but I think He already has."

Anton chuckled and slapped Emmitt on the shoulder. "I'd forgotten how kids have no filter, but I can't argue with him. Now we just have to convince her."

Yes, but Emmitt knew that would be the hard part. Mia had always been stubborn, and he'd given her good cause to distrust him. He'd thought they'd been reforging a connection yesterday but then she had pulled away again. What would it take to convince her that he'd changed for good?

CHAPTER FOURTEEN

"SO, how long have you and Anton been together?" Mia asked as they drove back to Emmitt's house. She had wanted to paint before they did anything else, so after moving the furniture to the middle of the room, they had driven to a local hardware store to pick up paint and supplies.

"Almost a year," Kris said as she pulled into the driveway. "He was the instructor in a nutrition class I took. It was love at first sight. For me at least."

"And for him?"

Kris shrugged as she placed the car in park. "I think it took him a little longer. He thought he wanted to play the field and keep his options open."

"What changed his mind?" Mia asked.

Kris turned off the engine and faced Mia. "Emmitt did,

actually. Evidently, he told Anton about how he'd lost the woman he loved when he'd listened to his teammates' advice to remain single. I can only assume he was talking about you."

"What do you mean?" Mia asked.

"Girl, are you crazy? I may not know you, but every girl in the world wishes they had a man who looked at them the way Emmitt looks at you. That man is clearly still in love with you."

"That man left me after he got drafted without a word. No goodbye, no closure, nothing. That's not how a man who loves a woman acts."

"Agreed," Kris said with a nod, "but it might be how a man who was influenced by friends might act."

Mia had never thought about the powerful influence of friends. She'd never been on a team, but she'd known enough people who had and they had often spoken about the family feel of being on a team. "But why wouldn't he reach out when he realized he was wrong?"

"Fear," Kris said. "Maybe he didn't know what to say. Maybe he felt guilty about the way he left. All I know is that I can guarantee you that Emmitt isn't that man anymore."

Mia wished she could be as certain as Kris, but she wasn't sure her heart could take rejection again. "Maybe you're right, but I'm not the same woman anymore either. Anyway, let's take the stuff inside. Perhaps we'll have a little time to paint before I have to take Carter to the hospital."

Kris said nothing more as she helped Mia unload the supplies and carry them in, but Mia could see the unspoken words on her face.

"Okay, bud, not a word to Mom about our plan. Do you think you can do that?" Emmitt asked as they finished unpacking the last box.

"Momma said it isn't good to keep secrets from her," Carter said, squeezing his dinosaur.

"He's got you there," Anton said with a laugh. He broke down the box and folded it flat.

Emmitt shot his friend a look before turning to Carter. "Your mom is right. You shouldn't keep secrets from her, but secrets are things you never tell. This is merely a surprise. We will tell her, but not until Christmas. Do you think you can keep from telling her until then?"

Carter puffed out his little chest. "Of course I can. I'm good at surprises."

"All right then. It's about time to head out for your appointment, so why don't we go grab your mom and if you feel up to it, we can get ice cream on the way home."

"Yes, ice cream. Will you come with us, Mr. Anton?"

"No, I've got some other things to do," Anton said as he picked up the stack of flattened boxes, "but I'll come see you tomorrow, and I'll be at the game Christmas Eve, okay, bud?"

"Sounds good," Carter said. "Maybe we can play more video games?"

"You bet." Anton turned to Emmitt. "I'm going to grab Kris too, but we'll both be by tomorrow before you head to practice. Let me know if you need anything else."

"Thank you," Emmitt said, "for everything."

Anton smiled and waved as he exited, and Emmitt turned to Carter. "Let's go get your mom."

They found Mia in the family room sealing up a can of paint. Tan splotches that matched the one painted wall dotted her hands and cheek. "Oh good, I was just about to come get you. Just let me wash up and we'll head out."

She dashed out of the room and Emmitt heard the sound of running water from the kitchen.

"Okay, I'm ready," she said when she reemerged.

Emmitt smiled and stepped closer to her. "Well, almost ready."

"What do you mean?" she asked. "Did I forget something?"

"You did. A little paint right here." Before she could move away, Emmitt reached up and brushed at the paint on her cheek. It didn't come off though, having dried to her cheek. "Well, that didn't go as I planned," he said with a chuckle.

Her eyes held his gaze, and he wanted to lean down and place his lips against hers, but Carter was watching. Mia broke contact and stepped back. "I'll be right back."

This time when she returned, the smear was gone, replaced with a red mark from scrubbing. "Okay, let's go."

Forty-five minutes later, they were following the doctor down the hall to the chemotherapy treatment room. Emmitt could sense the tension in Mia's shoulders, and he grabbed her hand. She glanced down at it and then back at him, but she didn't pull away.

"All right, big guy," Dr. Goodwin said when they reached the room. "Why don't you pick a chair and we'll get you all set up?"

Emmitt glanced around the room. It appeared to be divided by age with half of the room decorated with animals on the walls for the younger kids and the other half with superheroes for the older kids. There were recliners set about the room covered in colorful blankets and each one held a stuffed animal.

Carter hobbled over to a recliner that held a stuffed T-Rex. "I'll take this one."

"Good choice. Now, this is going to sting a little while we get your port in, but we have headphones with music you can listen to if you want."

"Okay, but can Momma hold my hand?"

Dr. Goodwin smiled and helped Carter into the chair.

"You bet, and your parents can stay with you the whole time."

As Mia didn't correct Dr. Goodwin, Emmitt didn't either. Instead, he squeezed her hand and offered a supportive smile.

"Okay, big guy, we just need to verify some information before we begin. Can you tell me your name?" Dr. Goodwin asked as Mia sat down beside Carter and grabbed his hand.

Carter giggled. "It's Carter Conrad."

"And how old are you?"

"I'm four." He held up his hand with his thumb folded down across his palm.

Dr. Goodwin smiled. "Okay, one more question. Do you know your birthday?"

"Yep, it's February eighth," he said proudly.

"Very good," she said.

Emmitt watched helplessly as a nurse joined Dr. Goodwin, and, after giving Carter a shot of anesthesia, they made an incision in his upper chest and inserted the port. The boy only grimaced once or twice, but Mia squeezed Emmitt's hand harder with each step. He was glad to be her support, but the whole procedure made his stomach turn. Emmitt didn't know how Mia could watch at all.

Once the port was in, the treatment began and Dr. Goodwin pulled over an additional chair for Emmitt. He sat there the entire hour watching Mia watch her son. What must that kind of love feel like? He knew he loved Mia, but loving her was different than loving a child. With every grimace on Carter's face, Mia would bite her lip and squeeze her eyes shut. Emmitt knew she must be holding back tears, and he wished he could do more for her.

MIA'S HEART broke as she put Carter to bed that evening. Dr. Goodwin had told her he might be tired, but he never went to sleep before nine. Here it was barely eight o'clock and he was already sound asleep in his bed.

Mia supposed she should be glad. At least asleep he felt no pain, and it allowed his body to heal. He hadn't talked about the procedure much on the way home, but she'd felt the pain with every grimace of his face. And even though she didn't want to lead him on, Mia had been grateful for Emmitt's presence. He'd said nothing the entire hour. Simply held her hand and watched in stoic silence. She was glad he didn't know Carter was his son right now because the pain of watching your child go through chemotherapy was excruciating, and while she knew she needed to tell him, she didn't want to ruin his last two games. No, it could wait until the season was over.

Satisfied that Carter probably wouldn't wake up again tonight, Mia left his room and wandered over to the main house. She wasn't even sure why. She had already thanked Emmitt at dinner, but the need to not be alone weighed heavy on her.

"Everything okay?" he asked when she found him in the living room. An open Bible filled his lap and reminded her that she hadn't spent nearly as much time in the Word as she should have recently.

"Yeah, I just didn't feel like being alone. Carter is asleep, and the silence was getting to me."

He patted the open couch next to him. "Want to join me in my devotional? Ironically, I'm in the book of Luke, chapter twelve."

"Why is that ironic?" she asked as she sat next to him. Her scripture memorization was obviously a little rusty.

He smiled at her. "Because it's all about trusting the Lord with our fear."

"Then I think I could definitely stand to hear it. Please read."

As Emmitt read the chapter aloud, Mia thought back to when they had dated. Though both had claimed to be Christians at the time, she couldn't remember a time they had read the Bible together. She wondered if their relationship might have been stronger if they had. She certainly felt stronger after listening to his deep voice read.

"Why did we never do this when we were dating?" she asked when he finished the chapter.

He sighed and closed the Bible before turning to her.

"Because I wasn't the man of God I should have been. I told you before that I thought I was a believer, and maybe I was, but I wasn't strong in my faith. I let the world influence my decisions too much—including the night with you. Had I been stronger, had we been doing this then, I would have made sure we waited until we were married.

"We would have done it right. I don't know about you, but while I will never say I didn't enjoy that night, I certainly didn't enjoy the guilt that consumed me after. It was what kept me away. I knew I had taken something from you that didn't belong to me, and I didn't know how to apologize. So I turned to God, and I grew in my faith. I didn't want to see you again until I was sure I could be the man you needed."

She should tell him. Right now. He had opened the door, and she should do the same. Apologize for not telling him about Carter, but she couldn't. Instead, she did the only thing she could think to do. She wound her arms around his neck and kissed him.

His body tensed momentarily, probably in surprise, and then he was kissing her back. Mia felt everything in that kiss —his hurt, his sorrow, his need for forgiveness—and she gave back what she could. She had no idea where this would leave them, but she knew that at this moment nothing felt more right than being in his arms.

"Come to my game Christmas Eve," he whispered into

her ear as the kiss ended. "I want you there with me. You and Carter both."

As he pushed her hair behind her ears and stared into her eyes, Mia knew that was what she wanted too. She wanted to be there to support him. She wanted to be his family. "If Carter feels up to it, then I promise we'll go."

CHAPTER FIFTEEN

FEBRUARY EIGHTH. Emmitt sat up in bed with wide eyes. *Could it be?* He tried to think back to high school health class. A pregnancy lasted nine months, right? *No, it was longer, but how much longer?* He needed his phone. His memory wasn't that good, and it was too early in the morning. He grabbed the phone from the nightstand and pressed the button to turn it on. Google would know. Clicking quickly to the app, he typed in *how long is a pregnancy?*

Forty weeks? So that was almost ten months. February was the second month so ten months back from that would be... He counted backward in his head. *April?*

April. The same month as the draft. The same month he and Mia had their one and only night together which meant that either she was with another man right before or right after Emmitt or...Carter was his son.

His son. Why hadn't she told him? Well, he knew the answer to that. He'd left without a word and never called her again. She probably thought he wouldn't care, but he did. The question now was did he tell her he knew? No, she must not want him to know yet. She probably wanted to be sure he would stick around this time, and he couldn't blame her. He could wait for her to tell him, but he had no idea if he'd be able to keep the smile off his face. He had a son.

"Well, you look like you had a nice break, Rev," Tucker Jackson said as Emmitt entered the locker room a few hours later.

"It didn't start out that way, but it is looking better." Emmitt smiled as he took off his tennis shoes and pulled out his cleats. "Has your break gotten any better?"

Tucker shrugged and tugged on his shoulder pads. "I'm still not excited about the trade, but at least I get to stay in Texas and I get to finish the season with the Saints. I'm trying to stay optimistic."

"That's good. Optimism is undervalued. Sometimes looking for the bright things in life will bring them to you." Emmitt pulled out his pads from the locker and donned them.

"Oh yeah? What got brought to you? Because you seem happier than normal. Not that you aren't normally happy, but you know what I mean."

Emmitt chuckled as he shrugged into his jersey. "I do know what you mean. God gave me a second chance with a woman I loved. I was young and stupid when I left her, and I've regretted it since. However, Matt made us promise to take care of our regrets over the break and those words gave me the courage to find her again. Now she's here and coming to the game tomorrow night." He didn't tell Tucker about his son though the words danced on the tip of his tongue. He wanted to shout the good news from the rooftop, but not until Mia confirmed it. Though he was ninety-nine percent positive, there was always the slim chance he was wrong.

"That's good, man. No regrets. Maybe I'll have to think about that. Anyway, see you out there."

"Yes, see you out there." Emmitt gave his body a final once over to make sure he was geared up and in regulations. Then he sat down on the bench to pray. It was something he did before every practice and every game. Though injuries were rare, when they did happen, they were usually series-ending and sometimes worse. So, he always prayed for safety for everyone on the team, and now, knowing he had a son, his safety was more important than ever before.

When he finished his prayer, he headed out onto the field for practice. There was a special peace that filled him when he was out on the field. Maybe it was the bigness of the stadium. Maybe it was the lights. Maybe it was the camaraderie with his teammates. Whatever it was, he enjoyed the time.

MIA SMILED at Kris as they finished painting the family room. Kris and Anton had arrived before Emmitt left for practice, and because Carter was still sleeping, Anton had offered to stay with him while Mia got to work.

"It's looking really good," Mia said as she surveyed the walls. So far, all they had done was paint, but the room already looked better, more complete. "I'd like to purchase some pillows and wall art. Do you think Anton will be okay with Carter for a little longer?"

"He will be fine," Kris said with a laugh. "This is like his dream—getting to play video games with a kid all day. I never play video games with him, but maybe I should."

"Do you think marriage is in your future?" Mia asked.

"I hope so. Seeing your son just makes me want kids even more." Kris pulled on her jacket and grabbed her keys.

Mia grabbed her jacket and purse from the table and followed Kris to the car. "Kids are amazing. Trying sometimes but amazing nonetheless. Even with everything going on, I wouldn't trade him for the world. Speaking of which, can we stop by a toy store as well? I'd like to pick up a few gifts for him."

"Of course," Kris said. "I bet Christmas is even more fun with kids."

Mia didn't tell her that the fun depended on your financial situation. Not that she needed to be wealthy, but it broke her heart when she couldn't even afford new clothes for Carter for Christmas, much less a toy that he might like. This year though, she was determined to get him something special with the advance Emmitt had given her. It would make it that much harder to pay the medical bills, but it would be worth it to see a smile on his face.

Carter was awake and playing games with Anton when Mia and Kris returned a few hours later.

"How are you feeling, buddy?" Mia asked as she set down her bags to give him a hug.

"Much better, Momma. I slept a lot, huh?" Though his voice was chipper, dark circles still ringed his eyes.

"You did, but Dr. Goodwin warned us you might. Did you get some food?" He had barely eaten anything after the treatment yesterday, and she worried he would get too skinny if he didn't eat more.

"Yeah, Anton made me the best mac n cheese before we started playing. You should have him teach you how."

Mia chuckled as she ruffled his hair. "I'll get right on that, dude. After I finish wrapping your Christmas gift. Unless you'd rather me spend the time learning how to make mac n cheese."

Carter's eyes lit up. "Is Christmas tomorrow?"

"No, tomorrow is Christmas Eve, but if you feel up to it, Mr. Emmitt has invited us to his game tomorrow night, and then we can open presents the next day."

"Yeah, I want to watch Mr. Emmitt play." He turned to Anton. "Will you be there too?"

Anton looked back to Kris, who nodded. "Yeah, buddy. Kris and I will be there too."

"All right, it's settled then," Mia said with a laugh. It felt good to laugh and see her son smile.

CHAPTER SIXTEEN

MIA'S JAW dropped as Emmitt led them into the luxury box. She'd always thought it was just seats behind a pane of glass in the middle of the field, but she'd been so wrong. There were chairs that sat near the glass, but there was also a wall of big screen TVs, couches and other plush chairs, a fully stocked bar, and a private bathroom.

"Wow, I understand the name now," Mia said as her eyes scanned the room.

"I'm glad you were able to come," Emmitt said, squeezing her hand. "I've often thought about having you watch the game from up here."

Mia flashed a teasing smile his direction. "Oh, you have, have you?"

"We get to watch the game from here?" Carter asked, interrupting the moment.

"You do, bud. I have to get down to the field to warm up soon, but Anton and Kris should be here shortly. Plus, there's a catering crew that works the game. You just let them know if you need anything."

Carter's eyes grew wide. "Anything?"

Emmitt chuckled. "Well, anything food or drink wise. They aren't Santa Claus, but he'll be coming tonight." He flashed a wink at Carter before turning to Mia again.

She could see that he wanted to kiss her, but she hadn't told Carter about them yet. Mia was fairly certain he wouldn't mind, but it was still something she wanted to discuss with him before he saw them kiss. So, she pulled him in for a hug instead and whispered in his ear, "I'll have a kiss for you after you win."

"You better," he returned, tickling her ear with his breath. "I'll see you guys after the game."

And then he was gone, and Mia and Carter were alone, but not for long. Soon, other people started filling the room. Mia felt completely out of her element as women dressed much nicer than her entered the room. She had worn her best skirt and shirt ensemble, but some of these women appeared more ready for a theater performance than a football game. Some appeared to know each other, but others shared her nervous expression. She wondered if they were other players' girlfriends or wives. Perhaps one day, she would get to know them, but for now she hoped Kris arrived soon so that she would at least have a friend to talk to.

"Mom, let's sit up here by the glass so we can see Mr. Emmitt," Carter called as he hobbled toward the chairs closest to the glass. He climbed up in one chair and Mia took the one next to him. Kris and Anton slid in next to her just before the game began.

"Sorry, we hit traffic," Kris whispered. "Did we miss the kickoff?"

Mia shook her head. She didn't think so, but she hadn't really watched football since Emmitt left.

"Which one is Mr. Emmitt?" Carter asked, squirming in his chair.

"He's number seventy-eight," Anton answered, "but I don't see him yet. Oh, wait, there he is."

Mia followed Anton's finger and after a moment, she was able to pick out number seventy-eight. She smiled with pride as she watched him tackle an opposing player. He really did look powerful and at home out on the field.

The game progressed quickly after that, and by halftime, the Saints were ahead but not by much, and anxiety coursed through Mia. Emmitt had told her they needed to win this game in order to make it to the championship game.

"I'm going to get something from the caterers. Can you stay here with Kris and Anton?" she asked Carter.

"Sure, this is fun." He had barely looked away from the field the whole first half. Mia had the sneaking suspicion that if he recovered from the osteosarcoma that she would have a football player on her hands in the next few years.

She made her way over to the bar and snagged one of the menus. As she scanned the offerings, the conversation from two women a few feet away carried over to her.

"They're playing much better," one woman said.

"They sure are. I bet it's because of their pact."

"Pact? What pact?"

"Andrew said the defensive linemen made a 'no-regrets' pact before the break. They were all to go make amends for their biggest regret. Maybe it cleared their heads and helped them to focus."

Mia looked over at the two women. One was blonde, the other brunette. They didn't appear upset by this so-called pact, but anger coursed through her. Was that the only reason Emmitt had come to Kempton? Was it not to apologize and seek forgiveness but to clear his head so he could play better? Was she simply a box to check off so they could win this game?

"Did you need something?" one of the caterers asked as he approached her.

"No, I don't think I'm hungry any longer," Mia said. She returned the menu to the counter and walked back to the chairs, but she suddenly had no desire to watch the rest of the game.

"What's wrong?" Kris asked, as if sensing her mood.

Mia shook her head. She couldn't believe she had fallen for Emmitt's act again, but she didn't trust herself to speak. At least, not yet.

EMMITT COULDN'T CONTAIN his smile as he headed up to the box to get Mia and Carter. Having them there had spurred him to play his best game ever, and he couldn't wait to hear what they thought.

"You did it, Mr. Emmitt," Carter said as soon as he saw him. "I watched the whole game."

Emmitt held his hand up for a high five from the boy—his son. Now that he knew, he could see his features in Carter's face—his eyes for sure. He wondered how he didn't see them at first. "You did? That's awesome. I think I played better because you were watching."

"Hmph," Mia said as Carter smacked his hand.

Emmitt turned to her, prepared to flash a smile, but it died on his face. Mia's expression was grim, and he wondered what had happened. Had someone been rude to her? He didn't know all the people who used the luxury box, but he thought most of them were nice.

"Is everything okay?" he asked her and reached for her hand.

"Fine. Let's just go home." Her words were short and she moved her hand out of his reach. Something had definitely happened, but the question was what?

"Okay, let me just say goodbye to Anton and Kris." He looked around for them but neither were in sight. Had something happened between them then?

"They've already gone. Said they had something they had to do tonight."

Right. It was eight o'clock on Christmas Eve. They had probably had plans with his parents. Emmitt was pretty sure Anton's folks celebrated Christmas Eve instead of Christmas Day. "All right then. I'm ready."

Mia nodded and walked past him. The ice she left in her wake chilled him to the bone. Trying not to worry, he took Carter's hand and helped him hobble back out to the car. Though Carter prattled on most of the ride home, the mood in the front remained tense. Emmitt knew he would have to get Mia alone to pry the answer out of her. And he would need to do it soon or the gift he had bought to give her tomorrow would have zero meaning.

"Can I help you put Carter to bed?" Emmitt asked when they arrived back at the guesthouse.

"I think we'll be fine," she said, stepping out of the vehicle before he could open the door for her.

"I want Mr. Emmitt to read to me tonight," Carter said from the back seat.

"Fine. I'll get you ready and he can read to you."

Emmitt felt like a third wheel as he watched Mia get Carter ready for bed. It was clear she wanted nothing to do with him, but he had no idea why. When Carter was in his pajamas, Mia kissed him and then sailed out of the room without even a side glance at Emmitt.

"Okay, buddy, what do you want to read?" Emmitt

asked as he looked around at the few books. He would have to get Carter more books. He wanted his son to be the reader he never was.

"The Cat in the Hat," Carter said with a yawn.

Emmitt opened the book and began reading the famous story. Before he was halfway through, Carter's eyes were closed and his chest rose and fell. Though Emmitt could have watched him sleep all night, he knew he had to find out what was bothering Mia first. He laid the book on the floor and then walked softly out of the room.

"Do you want to tell me what's going on?" Emmitt asked as he approached Mia.

Anger flashed in her eyes as she folded her arms across her chest. "Were you going to tell me about the pact?"

"Pact?" For a moment he was confused.

"Yeah, the pact. The 'no regrets pact' you guys made so you could clear your heads and win your last two games?" She made angry air quotes with her fingers as she said the words "no regrets."

"That wasn't what it was about," Emmitt said.

"Oh really? Why don't you tell me what it was about then?" She leaned against the counter and fixed him with an icy stare.

"It was about Diana. When she died, it affected all of us —perhaps Matt the most. Diana had always lived life to the fullest, so Matt wanted to do something in honor of her. He decided he would go home and fix the biggest regret of his past, and he challenged us to do the same."

"So I was a challenge? I can't believe I fell for you again."

Emmitt let out a frustrated breath. She had this all wrong, but he was afraid he wasn't explaining it well at all. "You weren't the challenge. The challenge was simply the push I needed to make the trip. I'd wanted to apologize to you for years, but I had no idea how."

"So what you're saying is that if it hadn't been for the pact, you still wouldn't have had the courage to apologize to me."

"I don't..." Emmitt fumbled over his words. He didn't understand why she was so angry. "Why does it matter what brought us back together?"

"It matters because I needed it to be me. I needed to know you were with me because you wanted to be and not because the guys convinced you to apologize to me."

"Is that why you didn't tell me Carter was my son?" The words came out before Emmitt could stop them. He had said he would wait for her to tell him, but it was too late now. "Because you wanted to make sure I was with you for you and not because I felt cornered?"

Her eyes widened. "When did you...?"

"Yesterday morning. When the doctor asked him his birthdate at the hospital, it stuck with me, but I couldn't figure out why. Then yesterday I woke up with this crazy idea that a February birthday might make conception really close to April. I googled it to be sure and figured he was either my child or you were with Marcus right after we were together. I couldn't fathom that possibility, and the more I looked at Carter, the more I realized. He has my eyes and my dimple."

Suddenly the fire left Mia and she sagged against the counter. "I'm sorry. I should have told you sooner. It all happened so quickly. You left without a word and then I found out I was pregnant. I met Marcus shortly after that, and though he knew I still loved you and was pregnant with your child, he offered to marry me and raise Carter as his own. I couldn't say no."

Emmitt crossed the space between them and pulled her into his arms. "Mia, you did what you thought was right. I don't blame you. We both made mistakes back then, but we don't have to keep making them now." He pushed a strand of hair behind her ear and cupped her chin so her eyes were locked on his. "Should I have come to apologize sooner? Yes, but I'm glad the pact spurred me to find you. Should you have told me five years ago you were pregnant? Yes, but I understand why you didn't."

"You're not angry?" she asked in a small voice.

"I am a little angry but not at you. I'm angry at myself. Angry that I left the way I did and that I didn't reach out to you sooner, but even more than that, I'm sad. Sad that I missed the first four years of Carter's life. I don't want to miss any more. I don't want to spend one more day without the two of you in my life. Please, tell me you can forgive me."

Tears spilled down Mia's face and she nodded. That was all the confirmation Emmitt needed. He pulled Mia to him and placed his lips on hers. That kiss said more than words ever could anyway. It asked forgiveness, it accepted apologies, and it healed the last five years.

When they pulled back, he looked down at her. "What do you say we wrap some presents for our son?" he asked as he wiped the wet sheen from Mia's cheek. She smiled and nodded, and Emmitt knew this would be his best Christmas ever.

CHAPTER SEVENTEEN

CHRISTMAS MORNING DAWNED early for Mia, but she didn't mind. For the first time in months, she was actually looking forward to Christmas. She and Emmitt had wrapped the gifts for Carter the night before and though it was more than he usually received, Mia was thankful Emmitt hadn't gone crazy. She didn't want Carter equating money with gifts.

"Momma, let's go open presents," Carter said again from the side of her bed. This time he added an arm shake.

"Okay, buddy, just give me a second to get my eyes open." She yawned and blinked a few times, but finally she was able to keep her eyes on him.

"Let's go, Momma."

With a laugh, Mia pushed back the cover and stepped out of bed. She hoped her hair wasn't too much of a mess because she didn't think Carter was going to give her time to brush it or her teeth for that matter. Grabbing her robe as they left her room, she shrugged into it as they walked down the hallway.

The crisp morning air greeted them as they opened the front door, but thankfully, there was no snow on the ground. Not that it snowed often on Christmas Day in Texas, but it had happened in the past.

"Look, Momma, smoke," Carter said as he blew out a cloud.

"Yep, that means it's cold. Let's get inside before you freeze."

Mia hoped the sliding glass door would be open. She had forgotten to warn Emmitt how early kids got up on Christmas, but the door slid open.

"Emmitt might not be up yet, bud," she warned Carter as they walked toward the living room.

"Does that mean we'll have to wait to open presents?" he asked.

"It does, but I'll bet you'll have a stocking to check out." In fact, they had filled the stocking with books, small toys, and candy. Hopefully it would entertain him until Emmitt woke.

However, as they entered the living room, Mia stopped in surprise. Emmitt was not only awake but appeared to be waiting for them. A Santa hat sat atop his head and he wore a red and white sweatshirt over red sweats. "Merry Christmas you two."

"Merry Christmas, Mr. Emmitt," Carter said as he hobbled forward to hug Emmitt. Mia flashed a smile at Emmitt. They had agreed to wait until Carter was a little older to tell him that Emmitt was his birth father, but she knew it must be hard on him all the same.

"Merry Christmas, bud. You ready to open some presents?"

"Yeah!" Carter hollered and pumped his fist in the air.

"Good. Why don't you and your mom sit on the couch, and I'll bring the presents to you?"

Carter nodded and crawled up on the couch. Mia sat beside him and flashed another warm grin at Emmitt. He had really gone all out this morning. He brought over the first gift and Mia enjoyed watching Carter tear into the stack of books.

"Will you read these to me later, Mr. Emmitt?" he asked.

Emmitt laughed—a deep, rich laugh as Mia poked Carter in the shoulder. "And what am I? Chopped liver?"

"You can read too, Mom."

His next present was a stack of the newest kid-friendly movies. "To add to our collection," Mia said.

"Thank you, Mom."

Then came the clothes. Having always been tight on

money, Mia was a big proponent of the four gifts for Christmas —something they want, something they need, something to wear, something to read. True, movies weren't something he needed, but it had been such a hard year that she had relented and allowed two wants. Besides, the one thing he needed—a cancer-free bill of health—she couldn't supply him anyway.

Finally, came his final present—a new game for him to play. His eyes lit up as he pulled back the paper. "Wow, thank you Mom, but I don't have a gaming system. What happens when we have to go home?"

"Actually, can you hold that question for just a second, buddy?" Emmitt asked. He returned to the tree and grabbed a small box from underneath it. Then he returned and held it out to Mia.

"For me?" She hadn't had the money to get Emmitt anything, and she certainly hadn't expected anything in return.

He nodded. "Open it."

Mia tore off the wrapping paper and sucked in her breath when the black velvet was revealed. Her eyes shot to Emmitt's, but he said nothing—merely smiled and urged her to continue. With trembling fingers, she pulled back the lid and her hand flew to her mouth.

Emmitt dropped to his knees and took the box from her. He held the ring out to her. "Mia, I am so glad you came back into my life, and I can't imagine continuing without you and Carter. Will you marry me?"

"Momma, say yes. Then my Christmas will be perfect," Carter said, tugging on her arm.

Mia smiled as a chuckle escaped her lips. "Yes. I will marry you."

EMMITT COULDN'T STOP SMILING as he placed the ring on Mia's finger. He had never imagined when Matt asked them to deal with their old regrets that he would not only reunite with Mia but find out he was a father as well.

"I know it's Christmas, but I'd love to get married before the championship game. I want to introduce you to everyone as my wife, so if you are amenable, Anton could marry us in the next few days, and we could have a traditional wedding later when we have more time to plan."

Mia blinked at him, obviously in shock. "You want to get married in the next few days?"

He took both of her hands in his. "I do. We've lost five years. Let's not lose any more." He hoped she said yes, because he and Anton had already made plans. Anton had filled out the paperwork for his justice of the peace credentials online.

"I have nothing to wear. No bouquet. No ring for you."

"I'll take care of all of that. We can go pick out a dress in a few days and a bouquet. All you have to say is yes."

"Come on, Mom. Please say yes."

Mia looked over at her son, who stuck out his lip for good measure, and Emmitt had to bite his lips together to keep from laughing. "Okay, yes, let's do it," Mia said.

Emmitt couldn't fight the emotions running through his body. He pulled Mia up to his chest, wrapped his arms around her waist, and kissed her. Even though it wasn't a married kiss yet, in Emmitt's heart, he knew he had married her five years ago the night he had spent with her. And he knew that having survived what they had already, nothing was going to keep them apart this time.

"I'm afraid I didn't get you anything," Mia said when she pulled back.

"Yes, you did. You said yes. That's the best Christmas gift you could ever give me."

"Ever?" she asked with a teasing glint in her eyes.

He caught her innuendo and pulled her close once again. They would do it right this time, but like her, he wanted more children. And this time, he wanted to be there with her every step of the way.

CHAPTER EIGHTEEN

MIA STARED at her reflection in the mirror. Odd, how this wasn't her perfect dress - there hadn't been time to find the "perfect" dress - but she still felt this was right. Having already been married once before, her simple ivory dress held no frills, but it hugged her figure in all the right places and fell to the floor in a cascade of satin. The lace detail across the bodice accented her slender shoulders, and the heart-shaped cutout in the back hinted at her smooth back.

The dress was new, and the garter she wore on her left thigh was blue. Her shoes were old, but she was still missing something borrowed.

The dressing room door opened behind her, and her mother's head appeared. Relief flooded Mia. She hadn't been sure her parents would show up - they certainly hadn't been thrilled about the engagement notice or the timeline of the wedding. Her mother had even asked if she was pregnant again, but Mia couldn't fault them. They'd been through this once already, and she knew they were worried not only about her own future but Carter's as well.

"May I come in?" Her mother's voice was soft and held a note of apology.

"Of course. I'm so happy to see you."

Her mother entered, shutting the door behind her. "I may not be sure of this union, but I wouldn't miss it for the world. Now, before I say anything else, are you sure you want to go through with this?"

Mia smiled at her mother's apprehension. She'd had her doubts as well, but Emmitt had distilled every one of them day by day, and her love for him now consumed her, overshadowed only for her love for God and her son. "I'm sure, Mom. Emmitt's changed. He's the man we always thought he could be, and he's Carter's father. Nothing could be better than uniting this family."

Her mother nodded, and her lips split into a wide smile. "I just wanted to be sure." She reached into her purse and withdrew a box. "You look beautiful, but I bet you could use something borrowed, am I right?" She opened the lid to reveal a stunning string of pearls.

Mia gasped and blinked back the tears that stung her eyes. "Mom, it's perfect. Thank you."

"No crying now. If you start, then I'll start, and you know what happens when I start crying."

Mia chuckled and dabbed at her eyes as her mother took the pearls and placed them on her neck. Now, she felt complete. Her mother smiled behind her and squeezed her shoulders.

The door opened again and Kris appeared in the entrance. "Are you ready? Everything else is in place."

Mia turned and hugged her mother before grabbing her bouquet and nodding at Kris. "I'm ready."

Kris was her only bridesmaid, but that was fine with Mia. The two had become close in the last week, and she knew they would be friends for the foreseeable future. Emmitt had asked Anton to be his best man, and while he had invited his teammates, most hadn't been able to attend. Mia had worried that might bother him, but he hadn't seemed to mind.

As they reached the closed door of the small sanctuary, Mia couldn't help but grin. Carter stood absolutely still in a black suit, his eyes glued to the small white pillow in his hands.

"He hasn't looked away from it yet," Anton said, catching her eye and flashing a wink.

"I have to concentrate real careful, so I don't drop it," Carter said without looking up.

"You're doing great, buddy." Mia didn't have the heart to tell him that the ring on the pillow was just for show and that Anton had the real ring in his pocket.

"Well, I better go find my seat," her mother said, giving her a quick hug before darting inside the door.

"You ready to do this again, Dad?" Mia asked.

Her father smiled at her. "I'll do it as many times as needed to get it right."

"It's right this time, Dad. I know it."

The music changed then and Anton pulled the door open. Mia's eyes caught Emmitt's across the room, and the world around her grew silent. She was about to marry the man she had loved for as long as she could remember, and nothing else mattered.

**

Emmitt looked up as the back doors swung open. His eyes caught Mia's, and his breath stilled. She was a vision in her satin ivory dress. Her hair was piled on her head and accented with flowers, and a few tiny tendrils snaked around her ears. He couldn't wait to touch those tendrils.

Though he wanted nothing more than to keep his eyes on Mia, he forced his gaze to Carter, his son, who was walking down the aisle. Well, inching might have been a better word. The boy was moving slowly, and all his concentration was on the pillow in his hands. Emmitt bit his lips to keep from smiling, and a hushed titter of laughter scattered throughout the room.

When Carter finally reached the stage, he turned and smiled out at the audience, lifting his eyes for the first time. Only then, did Anton and Kris begin their walk.

And then it was Mia's turn. He kept his eyes on her until she was beside him and had handed her bouquet to Kris. Then he took her hands in his. He could feel their heartbeats pulsing in union, and he knew the rest of their life would be the same.

"Dearly beloved, we are gathered here today…"

He barely heard the rest of the preacher's words as Mia consumed his focus. Only when a cough sounded behind him did he turn to see Anton holding out the ring. Right. Vows. They needed to exchange vows before she would be completely his. He took the ring, repeated the preacher's words, and slipped the ring on her finger. She did the same for him, and as the gold band slid onto his finger, he finally felt the weight of his past mistakes ease off his shoulders.

Thank you, God, he thought as he looked up at the ceiling of the sanctuary. *Thank you for taking my mistake and turning it into a masterpiece.*

"I now pronounce you husband and wife. You may kiss the bride."

THE EPILOGUE

EMMITT THOUGHT his nerves had been on end before the championship game, but that was nothing compared to the fear, hope, and love coursing through him right now. They had won the game in the final two seconds, and that night had been euphoric. Hoisting Matt on his shoulders for the last time with Jordan, having Mia and Carter meet him on the field, introducing her to everyone as his wife had all been amazing life-changing memories, but this was so much more.

He grasped Mia's hand and squeezed. The eyes she turned on him swam with fear, but she forced a brave smile as she returned his squeeze. Today was the day they would find out the results of Carter's latest scan.

After ten weeks of treatment and countless nights with no sleep as one of them sat up with him or both of them prayed over him, he had undergone surgery to remove the tumor from his bone. Not the way he had wanted to celebrate his birthday, but the doctors had insisted they got it all. They even added that it had been a relatively small piece of his bone, which meant that while he would never play professional football like Emmitt, he might be able to walk without a limp, maybe even run.

But then there had been four more weeks of treatment. Those had been even harder because not only was Carter's body tired of the toxic chemicals coursing through him, but his young brain couldn't process the why. To him, the tumor had been removed, so why did he have to keep doing the thing that made him sick? Getting him to the hospital had been a constant battle, and nerves in the house had run high.

Dr. Goodwin closed the file and folded her hands together. She took a deep breath and then lifted her eyes to meet theirs. "Mr. and Mrs. Brown—"

Emmitt felt the invisible cord around his heart squeeze. He didn't think Mia and Carter could handle it if the news was bad, and not having a solution for them would tax him as well.

"I'm pleased to say that Carter's scans came back negative."

Negative? Did she say negative? Emmitt glanced over at Mia. Tears ran down her face and her shoulders bowed forward as if bearing a heavy burden. Was she happy? Sad?

"We will want to monitor him and re-scan every six

months, but for now I can say that Carter's cancer is in remission."

"Remission." The word felt like honey on his tongue. "He's cancer-free?"

Dr. Goodwin smiled and nodded. "He is."

"Praise God!"

"So no more treatments? No more chemo?" Mia's voice was quiet and small next to him.

"Not for now, and as long as his scans come back clean, he won't have to undergo them again."

"Thank you, Dr. Goodwin."

"You're very welcome. These appointments are my favorite by far. I'll give you a few minutes to process your emotions and then I'll be back with Carter."

As she left the room, an enormous sob escaped Mia's lips. Emmitt pulled her to his chest. He knew the emotions were of joy and not sadness, but he also knew she needed to let the tears fall.

He held her until the tears ceased, and then he wiped the traces from her cheek. "Are you ready to give Carter a hug?"

"Almost," she sniffed. "I just have to tell you one thing first."

Emmitt held his breath as the cord around his heart squeezed again. Did she have her own bad news? Had he misread her tears? "What is it?"

"We're pregnant."

With a cheerful laugh, Emmitt pulled her to her feet. Yes, winning the championship game had been amazing, but this day definitely took the cake.

"Momma, Daddy, I'm cancer free," Carter said as the door opened and he limped across the room to them.

"We know, buddy," Emmitt said, lifting him into the air. "What a glorious day!"

"It's the best day ever!" Carter said with a wide smile, and Emmitt couldn't agree more.

The End!

If you loved Emmitt and Mia's story, would you be willing to leave a review? Reviews help other readers find books they will enjoy.

And don't forget to turn the page for a sneak peek at Run with My Heart

AUTHOR'S NOTE

First off, let me say how glad I am that you read this book. I so enjoyed writing this series. So much so that I have three more football books planned. I hope you'll continue the journey by following Tucker Jackson to the Texas Tornados.

I've been a football fan since the age of four. I'm from Texas so football is king down there. I used to watch every Sunday with my father, and when I was in college, I actually got to attend a game at the old Cowboy stadium. I haven't made it to the new one yet, but it's on my bucket list.

I grew up watching football when the Dallas Cowboys were a powerhouse – Troy Aikman, Michael Irving, and of course my favorite Emmitt Smith. As I said in the note at the beginning, I loved Emmitt's drive and the fact that he earned a degree and didn't just rely on his football talent.

Turns out he's not a bad dancer either if you watched him win Dancing With the Stars.

So, if you've enjoyed reading this author's note so far (and really, how could you not?) I am offering, for today only, a page where you can sign up for my weekly newsletter for the low, low price of absolutely nothing.

Included in this weekly newsletter is many wonderful things like pictures of my adorable children, chances to win awesome prizes, new releases and sales I might be holding, great books from other authors, and anything else that strikes my fancy and that I think you would enjoy.

Even better, I solemnly swear to only send out one newsletter a week (usually on Tuesday unless life gets in the way which with three kids it often does). I will not spam you, sell your email address to solicitors or anyone else, or any of those other terrible things.

Join me here and receive the free short story as my thank-you gift for choosing to hang out with me. It's fun and entertaining. I promise.

Prayers and blessings,

Lorana

NOT READY TO SAY GOODBYE?

I introduced Tucker Jackson in this book, so let me tell you a little more about his story.

Tucker Jackson thought getting traded was the worst thing that could happen to him. But after getting caught in a bar brawl, he is sentenced to community service. He was supposed to be helping kids, not falling in love with the feisty director.

Shelby Doll loves her job but she hates working with all the athletes that get sent over and Tucker Jackson is no exception. The chip on his shoulder is nearly as big as his ego and it takes all her control not to kick him to the curb. But when he bonds with the most unlikely of kids, will she see him in a different light?

19

RUN WITH MY HEART PREVIEW

TUCKER JACKSON WATCHED as the clock ran out, and his hand curled into a fist at his side. Three points. They had lost by three points. He knew they were in the tougher part of their schedule, but if they kept losing like this, they would lose their spot in the playoffs. They were already sitting in wild card position. One more loss, and they would be out. Their season would be done.

As he slapped hands with the opposing team members, he thought again of the trade that had landed him here. Last year at this time, he had been on the Saints. Sure, he hadn't gotten to play much, but the Saints had won the Championship game. He even had the ring to prove it, although it didn't mean as much as it might have because he'd known even then he was getting traded to the Texas Tornados.

Trades happened in football. All the time. But why did

it have to happen to him? He hadn't even gotten the chance to show the Saints what he could do. And yes, the Tornados were letting him run more, but what good was that if they didn't win?

He finished the congratulatory line and headed into the locker room. Carter Chapman, quarterback, captain, and longest team member stood at the door smiling and patting the guys as they entered.

"Good game," Carter Chapman said clapping Tucker on the shoulder. "We'll get them next time." Chapman was a good guy, but he was always spouting platitudes like these. Tucker was tired of his optimism.

"Will we?" Tucker asked, his voice dripping with condescension. "If we lose the next game, we're out for the rest of the season. If you had just let me run that last play..."

Carter shook his head and fixed his steely eyes on Tucker. His voice dropped to his serious captain's voice - the one that declared he was in charge. "I made a call. They were all over your running game today. Maybe it would have played out differently if you had run, but maybe not. We can't win every game, Tucker, and if you only focus on the ones we lose, you will never find the joy of playing the game."

"Is that what you guys told yourselves when you lost out last year?" Tucker stared defiantly at Carter. He knew Carter wasn't to blame for their loss last year. There were a lot of teams and only two made it to the championship game, but he couldn't seem to tame the anger coursing through his veins.

"Shower and get out of here," Carter said. "You need some time off." Though his words were forceful, and his gaze backed them up, he didn't raise his voice or yell. Tucker might have felt better if he had.

"Carter, I'm sorry man. I'm just frustrated." Tucker knew he had stepped over the line, and if he didn't get back in Carter's good graces, he'd be riding the bench and probably facing another trade.

"We all are, but I wasn't kidding. Go clear your head and decide if this is still where you want to be. What you want to be doing. IF it is, I'll see you at practice at five pm."

Tucker knew better than to argue. Like a scolded puppy, he hung his head and shuffled past Carter, barely managing a "Yes, sir." He berated himself as he walked to his locker. His temper was getting the better of him again, and he needed to get it under control.

Around him, his teammates bantered back and forth. Some spouted their favorite plays of the game. Some bemoaned mistakes they had made. But they all appeared in better spirits than Tucker. Why did he always turn to anger? Why did he always focus on the worst-case scenario?

**

Shelby Doll stared out at the kids playing in the old gymnasium and sighed.

"Uh oh, I know that sigh," her friend Kenzie said beside her. "What's wrong?"

"What's always wrong?" Shelby asked shaking her head. "Money. The rent is due on this place by the end of the month, and we don't have it. Attendance has dropped since that trampoline park opened up down the street."

"That place is just a fad," Kenzie said with a wave of her hand. "It won't last, and when kids tire of it, they'll come back here because you are amazing."

Shelby didn't know about that. When she had begun running the center five years ago, she felt amazing, but now she felt... Behind the times. "What if they don't? Those kids out there need us." Her eyes found Darby, a young girl with glasses bigger than her face whose father had just been killed in the line of duty. Her mother needed this place for Darby, but she was strapped financially now that she was a single mother. And then there was Quinn. Tall and skinny, he was often picked on at school because he spent more time reading than playing sports or the newest video game. But here he was just one of the gang. His mother was battling cancer, so there was no extra money there. And then there was Brayden. She still wasn't sure exactly how he had become paralyzed as he never talked about it, but his mother had left when he was young, and his father worked long hours.

There were other kids, but these three always stood out to her because they seemed to need the center the most. She scanned the gymnasium again. Once, they had watched nearly every school age kid for at least a few hours. Basketballs would echo across the floor as teams played. One corner of the gym had once been staked out for reading and playing cards. Still another part had been the creative hangout for students who enjoyed theater and role play. But then the trampoline park had opened and offered a discounted rate for kids needing only a few hours after school. It had been lower than Shelby could afford to charge, and many of the kids had left.

Now, there were only a handful. A few basketballs still thudded against the floor, but the sound was sad as if even the kids couldn't muster the emotion of delight that had previously lived there. Now, most of the kids read or worked on homework, and the muted atmosphere broke Shelby's heart.

"What if they don't?" she asked again. "What if, come the new year, we can't pay the rent, and we have to close the doors forever?"

Kenzie flashed a sympathetic smile as she wrapped an arm around Shelby's shoulders. "We'll just have to pray that doesn't happen."

A FREE STORY FOR YOU!

Enjoyed this story? Not ready to quit reading yet? If you sign up for my newsletter, you will receive The Billionaire's Impromptu Bet right away as my thank you gift for choosing to hang out with me.

A SWAT officer. A bored billionaire heiress. A bet that could change everything....

Read on for a taste of The Billionaire's Impromptu Bet....

THE BILLIONAIRE'S IMPROMPTU BET PREVIEW

Brie Carter fell back spread eagle on her queen-sized canopy bed sending her blonde hair fanning out behind her. With a large sigh, she uttered, "I'm bored."

"How can you be bored? You have like millions of dollars." Her friend, Ariel, plopped down in a seated position on the bed beside her and flicked her raven hair off her shoulder. "You want to go shopping? I hear Tiffany's is having a special right now."

Brie rolled her eyes. Shopping? Where was the excitement in that? With her three platinum cards, she could go shopping whenever she wanted. "No, I'm bored with shopping too. I have everything. I want to do something exciting. Something we don't normally do."

Brie enjoyed being rich. She loved the unlimited credit cards at her disposal, the constant apparel of new clothes, and of course the penthouse apartment her father paid for, but lately, she longed for something more fulfilling.

Ariel's hazel eyes widened. "I know. There's a new bar down on Franklin Street. Why don't we go play a little game?"

Brie sat up, intrigued at the secrecy and the twinkle in Ariel's eyes. "What kind of game?"

"A betting game. You let me pick out any man in the place. Then you try to get him to propose to you."

Brie wrinkled her nose. "But I don't want to get married." She loved her freedom and didn't want to share her penthouse with anyone, especially some man.

"You don't marry him, silly. You just get him to propose."

Brie bit her lip as she thought. It had been awhile since her last relationship and having a man dote on her for a month might be interesting, but…. "I don't know. It doesn't seem very nice."

"How about I sweeten the pot? If you win, I'll set you up on a date with my brother."

Brie cocked her head. Was she serious? The only thing Brie couldn't seem to buy in the world was the affection of Ariel's very handsome, very wealthy, brother. He was a movie star, just the kind of person Brie could consider marrying in the future. She'd had a crush on him as long as she and Ariel had been friends, but he'd always seen her as just that, his little sister's friend. "I thought you didn't want me dating your brother."

"I don't." Ariel shrugged. "But he's between girlfriends right now, and I know you've wanted it for ages. If you win this bet, I'll set you up. I can't guarantee any more than one date though. The rest will be up to you."

Brie wasn't worried about that. Charm she possessed in abundance. She simply needed some alone time with him, and she was certain she'd be able to convince him they were meant to be together. "All right. You've got a deal."

Ariel smiled. "Perfect. Let's get you changed then and see who the lucky man will be.

A tiny tug pulled on Brie's heart that this still wasn't right, but she dismissed it. This was simply a means to an end, and he'd never have to know.

Jesse Calhoun relaxed as the rhythmic thudding of the speed bag reached his ears. Though he loved his job, it was stressful being the SWAT sniper. He hated having to take human lives and today had been especially rough. The team had been called out to a drug bust, and Jesse was forced to return fire at three hostiles. He didn't care that they fired at his team and himself first. Taking a life was always hard, and every one of them haunted his dreams.

"You gonna bust that one too?" His co-worker Brendan

appeared by his side. Brendan was the opposite of Jesse in nearly every way. Where Jesse's hair was a dark copper, Brendan's was nearly black. Jesse sported paler skin and a dusting of freckles across his nose, but Brendan's skin was naturally dark and freckle free.

Jesse flashed a crooked grin, but kept his eyes on the small, swinging black bag. The speed bag was his way to release, but a few times he had started hitting while still too keyed up and he had ruptured the bag. Okay, five times, but who was counting really? Besides, it was a better way to calm his nerves than other things he could choose. Drinking, fights, gambling, women.

"Nah, I think this one will last a little longer." His shoulders began to burn, and he gave the bag another few punches for good measure before dropping his arms and letting it swing to a stop. "See? It lives to be hit at least another day." Every once in a while, Jesse missed training the way he used to. Before he joined the force, he had been an amateur boxer, on his way to being a pro, but a shoulder injury had delayed his training and forced him to consider something else. It had eventually healed, but by then he had lost his edge.

"Hey, why don't you come drink with us?" Brendan clapped a hand on Jesse's shoulder as they headed into the locker room.

"You know I don't drink." Jesse often felt like the outsider of the team. While half of the six-man team was married, the other half found solace in empty bottles and meaningless relationships. Jesse understood that - their job was such that they never knew if they would come home night after night - but he still couldn't partake.

Brendan opened his locker and pulled out a clean shirt. He peeled off his current one and added deodorant before tugging on the new one. "You don't have to drink. Look, I won't drink either. Just come and hang out with us. You have no one waiting for you at home."

That wasn't entirely true. Jesse had Bugsy, his Boston Terrier, but he understood Brendan's point. Most days, Jesse went home, fed Bugsy, made dinner, and fell asleep watching TV on the couch. It wasn't much of a life. "All right, I'll go, but I'm not drinking."

Brendan's lips pulled back to reveal his perfectly white teeth. He bragged about them, but Jesse knew they were veneers. "That's the spirit. Hurry up and change. We don't want to leave the rest of the team waiting."

"Is everyone coming?" Jesse pulled out his shower necessities. Brendan might feel comfortable going out with just a new application of deodorant, but Jesse needed to wash more than just dirt and sweat off. He needed to wash the sound of the bullets and the sight of lifeless bodies from his mind.

"Yeah, Pat's wife is pregnant again and demanding some crazy food concoctions. Pat agreed to pick them up if she let him have an hour. Cam and Jared's wives are having a girls' night, so the whole gang can be together. It will be nice to hang out when we aren't worried about being shot at."

"Fine. Give me ten minutes. Unlike you, I like to clean up before I go out."

Brendan smirked. "I've never had any complaints. Besides, do you know how long it takes me to get my hair like this?"

Jesse shook his head as he walked into the shower, but he knew it was true. Brendan had rugged good looks and muscles to match. He rarely had a hard time finding a woman. Jesse on the other hand hadn't dated anyone in the last few months. It wasn't that he hadn't been looking, but he was quieter than his teammates. And he wasn't looking for right now. He was looking for forever. He just hadn't found it yet.

Click here to continue reading The Billionaire's Impromptu Bet.

THE STORY DOESN'T END

You've met a few people and fallen in love.... I bet you're wondering how you can meet everyone else.

Star Lake Series:

When Love Returns: Presley Hays and Brandon Scott were best friends in High School until Morgan entered their town and stole Brandon's heart. Can Presley and Brandon forget past hurts or will their stubborn natures keep them apart forever?

Once Upon a Star: Audrey left Star Lake to pursue acting, but after an unplanned pregnancy her jobs and her money dwindled, leaving her no option except to return home and start over. Once Upon a Star will take you back to Christmas in Star Lake.

Love Conquers All: Lanie Perkins Hall never imagined being divorced at thirty. Azarius Jacobson has loved Lanie Perkins Hall from the moment he saw her, but issues from his past have left him guarded.

The Heartbeats Series:

Where It All Began: Sandra Baker thought her life was on the right track until she ended up pregnant. Will she tell Henry her darkest secret? And will she ever be able to forgive herself and find healing? Find out in this emotional love story.

The Power of Prayer: Callie Green thought she had her whole life planned out until her fiance left her at the altar. Who will she choose and how will her choice affect the rest of her life? Find out in this touching novel.

When Hearts Collide: Amanda Adams has always been a Christian, but she's a novice at relationships. She captivates his heart, but can he save her from making the biggest mistake of her life?

A Past Forgiven: Jess Peterson has lived a life of abuse and lost her self worth, but when she is paired with a Christian roommate, she begins to wonder if there is a loving father looking down on her. Can the man in her life step up and be there for Jess and the baby?

Sweet Billionaires Series:

The Billionaire's Secret: Maxwell Banks was the ultimate player until he found himself caring for a daughter he didn't know he had. Can he change to become the role model she needs?

A Brush with a Billionaire: Brent just wanted to finish his novel in peace, but when his car breaks down in Sweet Grove, he is forced to deal with a female mechanic and try to get along.

The Billionaire's Christmas Miracle: Drew Devonshire is captivated by the woman he meets at a masquerade ball, but who is she?

The Billionaire's Cowboy Groom: Carrie Bliss finally found the man she wants to marry but there's just one little problem.

The Cowboy Billionaire: Coming Soon!

The Lawkeeper Series:

Lawfully Matched: Kate Whidby doesn't want to impose on her newly married brother after their parents die, so she accepts a mail order bride offer in the paper.

Lawfully Justified: William Cook turns to bounty hunting after losing his wife. Can William find a way to heal from his broken past to start a future with Emma? Or will a haunting secret take away all the possibilities of this budding romance?

The Scarlet Wedding: William and Emma are planning their wedding, but an outbreak and a return from his past force them to change their plans. Is a happily ever after still in their future?

Lawfully Redeemed: Dani Higgins is a K9 cop looking to make a name for herself, but she finds herself at the mercy of a stranger after an accident.

The Still Small Voice Series:
The Still Small Voice: Jordan Wright was searching for something after she gave her son up for adoption. What she found was God, and she began receiving visions. Will she be able to give up control and do what is asked of her?
A Spark in the Darkness coming soon!

Blushing Brides Series:
The Cowboy's Reality Bride: Tyler Hall just wanted to find love, but the women he dated wanted more than his small-town life provided. He gets more than he bargained for when he ends up on a reality dating show and falls for a woman who is not a contestant.
The Reality Bride's Baby: Laney wants nothing more than a baby, but when she starts feeling dizzy is it pregnancy or something more serious?
The Producer's Unlikely Bride: Justin Miller had given up on love, but when his image needs help, he finds himself needing the aid of a stranger who just happens to be a romance writer.
Ava's Blessing in Disguise: Five years after marriage, Ava faces a mysterious illness that threatens to ruin her career. Will she find out what it is?

The Soldier's Steadfast Bride: coming soon

The Men of Fire Beach

Fire Games: Cassidy returns home from Who Wants to Marry a Cowboy to find obsessive letters from a fan. The cop assigned to help her wants to get back to his case, but what she sees at a fire may just be the key he's looking for.

Lost Memories and New Beginnings: She wants to remember who she is after the accident, but when pieces begin to fall into place that point to a troubled past, will she be able to convince Brody she's changed?

When Questions Abound: The companion guide to Lost Memories. This short story gives the point of view from the cop who is investigating.

Never Forget the Past: A mysterious woman from Bubba Campbell's past has just shown up and uprooted his life. Who is this woman and why has he been using a different name?

Stand Alones:

Love Renewed: This books is part of the multi author second chance series. When fate reunites high school sweethearts separated by life's choices, can they find a second chance at love at a snowy lodge amid a little mystery?

Her children's early reader chapter book series:

The Wishing Stone #1: Dangerous Dinosaur

The Wishing Stone #2: Dragon Dilemma

The Wishing Stone #3: Mesmerizing Mermaids

The Wishing Stone #4: Pyramid Puzzle

The Wishing Stone Inspirations 1: Mary's Miracle

To see a list of all her books

authorloranahoopes.com

loranahoopes@gmail.com

ABOUT THE AUTHOR

Lorana Hoopes is an inspirational author originally from Texas but now living in the PNW with her husband and three children. When not writing, she can be seen kick-boxing at the gym, singing, or acting on stage. One day, she hopes to retire from teaching and write full time.

facebook.com/loranalhoopes

twitter.com/LoranaHoopes

instagram.com/authorloranahoopes

bookbub.com/authors/lorana-hoopes

goodreads.com/author/show/15197780.Lorana_Hoopes_L-L_Hoopes_